Kindred Spirits

slaves · seminoles · freedom · war

Kindred Spirits

slaves · seminoles · freedom · war

kevin christopher
brown

Jacket concept by Abby Bordner
Jacket design by Kevin Brown Studio
Back cover photograph © Dana Waldon

Also by

Kevin Christopher Brown

Stupid Sh*t We Did in College... (and stuff)

For my mother,

Jacqueline Elizabeth Narcisse Brown

rest in peace

LE CODE NOIR

THE CIVIL CODE OF LOUISIANA

Art. 16—Slaves belonging to different masters must not gather at any time under any circumstance.

Art. 33—A slave who struck his or her master, his wife, mistress or children would be executed.

Art. 35—A slave is one who is in the power of a master to whom he belongs. The master may sell him, dispose of his person, his industry, and his labor: he can do nothing, possess nothing, nor acquire anything but what must belong to his master.

Art. 42—Masters may chain and beat slaves but may not torture nor mutilate them.

Art. 47—A slave husband and wife (and their prepubescent children under the age of 10 years) belonging to the same master were not to be sold separately.

Art. 55—Slave masters 20 years of age may free their slaves.

Art. 95—Free persons and slaves are incapable of contracting marriage together. There is the same incapacity and the same nullity with respect to marriages contracted by free white persons with free people of color.

Art. 182—Slaves cannot marry without the consent of their masters, and their marriages do not produce any of the civil effects which result from such a contract.

Art. 183—Children born of a mother then in a state of slavery, whether married or not, follow the condition of their mother; they are consequently slaves, and belong to the master of their mother.

Art. 185—No one can emancipate his slave unless the slave has attained the age of thirty years, and has behaved well at least four years preceding his emancipation.

Art. 226—Illegitimate children, who have not been legally acknowledged, may be allowed to prove their paternal descent, provided they be free and white.

Art. 492—The children of slaves and the young of animals belong to the proprietor of the mother of them, by right of accession.

Art. 537—Natural fruits are such as are the spontaneous produce of earth; the produce and increase of cattle, and the children of slaves are likewise natural fruits.

Art. 631—He who has the use of one or more slaves or animals has the right to enjoy their service for his wants and those of his family.

Art. 945—All free persons, even minors, lunatics, persons of insane mind and the like, may transmit their estates ab intestato and inherit from others. Slaves alone are incapable of either.

That peace only came in death.

—Slave, Whitney Plantation
St. John the Baptist Parish, Louisiana

I

FLORIDA WILDERNESS · AUGUST · 1853

A steamy mist hung on the quiet dawn stillness. A vast, unforgiving wilderness, rugged and untamed, thousands of years in the making. The lush tapestry of palmettos, ferns, and countless other plants growing from the marshy ground gave way to towering cypress trees and broad majestic oaks; timeworn trees whose craggy branches sagged low under their tremendous weight, meeting the

1

ground in places, reconnecting them to the land whence they came. Gray-green Spanish moss floated softly in fair abundance from tree limbs, heightening the eeriness of a place unseen by civilized eyes, lost in time. America was still uncharted, except by the native people who had been hammering out a rugged existence in the country for centuries—people intimately familiar with every stretch of the landscape, like they would the back of their hand. Long ago these pathfinders scoured the country's terrain and discovered its epic beauty and its bounty, bravely crossing broad rivers and deep crystalline lakes, descending into its many grand valleys. First to discover America's abundant wildlife, they had traversed rugged snowcapped mountains, high mesas and deep canyons, fearlessly forging trails across vast deserts, immense plains, and through remote forests. This was their land.

As the day wore on, minutes dragging into hours, morning dragging into afternoon and the temperature steadily rising, opportunistic shafts of light found their way through the thick leafy canopy, painting small patches of forest yellow. The place teemed with wildlife, yet mosquitos seemed the only creatures willing to stir in the sweltering heat—mosquitos … and the dragonflies that hunted them. The suffocating humidity added still another layer of difficulty to this inhospitable wilderness. It was a merciless place where time moved at its own slow, languid pace. Somewhere off in the distance, over the cacophony of silence, a faint sound echoed, building slowly through the undulating haze … breaking the ancient forest's code of silence.

From the coolness of its underground

lair, a small gray fox stirred, trembling nervously in the thick undergrowth, instinctively fearful of the echoes growing in the distance. Its moist black nose poked through the undergrowth, followed by its slight frame, pointed ears perking up to funnel in the strange sounds—noises wholly unfamiliar to the fox's heightened sense of sound and pinpoint hearing honed over thousands of millennia. The strange noises weren't the only thing that held the fox in a state of alarm. It felt the earth tremble up through its legs and down its spine as it detected the faintest trace of an unusual odor, causing its nose to agitate and its bushy black-tipped tail to twitch with fear.

The hunting dogs sensed they were close. Their barking grew excited and frenzied, their salivary glands fully activated. They couldn't see it yet, but the 230 million olfactory cells in their noses told them their quarry was near. Through the din of barking dogs, a low, rumbling vibration grew slowly and steadily to a thunderous crescendo. Its senses overwhelmed, the fox froze, paralyzed with fear, the hairs running down its spine forming a bristly mohawk as they stood on end.

Six white horsemen wove as quickly as their horses could maneuver through the maze of trees and undergrowth, their bodies twisting and ducking in unison with their horses. The rough-hewn men's clothes were sullied and sticky with sweat, and their scruffy, weathered faces bore a focused determination—an overwhelming desire to overcome the brutal environment, get what they had come for, and get the hell out. Armed and dangerous and full of bad intentions, these men were—men who had journeyed far too long to lose their prize and much too far to accept failure. Given their ragged, roughshod appearance and uncouth nature, it was understandable to assume the horses they rode were ill-gotten. That assumption would prove incorrect. These were not common criminals or simple horse thieves but rather vandals of a more sinister, much viler nature.

Riding out front and leading this unkempt posse was John Clay, who despite his current appearance was more genteel than the others and whose grayed temples indicated he was in the middle stages of his life. His friends called him Jack. Everyone else called him *Master* Jack. Following just behind Master Jack was the rest of his posse of roughriders: Austin, LaSalle, Boudreaux, Smith, and Guidry. Their horses thundered through the forest, nostrils flaring wide, sucking in as much oxygen as their lungs could hold, hooves pounding the moist turf. The fifteen or so bloodhounds set the pace. Ripe with anticipation and excitement, the dogs were seemingly immune to both fatigue and peril, running unfazed amongst the horses, deftly avoiding the crushing hooves as they weaved through the trees and undergrowth. As the posse stormed closer and the crescendo of sound grew, the fox's survival instincts kicked in. Compelled by its eagerness to survive, the fox bolted into the open … and ran for its life.

LaSalle was ornery and squint-eyed, the crooked scowl he wore permanently embedded on his face, a compliment to the jagged scar running down the opposite cheek. The guy nobody fucked with—even the members of his own posse. He was a moody, ill-tempered, cold-blooded son-of-a-bitch all right, but his slight derangement was really why most people steered clear. Better safe than sorry with this guy. It was hard to imagine LaSalle having any semblance of a childhood, let alone a decent one, and he enjoyed punishing people for it every chance he got—his personal form of retribution to his unfit, uninterested, half-assed parents. No more than a child when he left his strife-ridden home, LaSalle was more apt to confide in a squirrel than a human being, and his penchant for verbally abusing people was second only to his appetite for physically assaulting them.

As the posse twisted its way through the forest and the fox made its panicked escape, LaSalle snatched a black Colt Walker from his hip and deftly tilted it skyward, his greasy thumb cocking the trigger. In one smooth motion, he pointed, aimed … *BOOM!* A thundering blast exploded from the barrel, the white gun smoke that followed billowing from the chamber, wafting into the thick, muggy air. Satisfied with his shot, LaSalle spun the fifteen-inch single-action revolver around his index finger once then slammed it back into its black holster. Then he allowed himself the satisfaction of a sinister self-satisfied grin.

2

Mercy was running in sheer desperation, as fast as her exhaustion would allow, when the .44 caliber lead bullet exploded into her back. The force from the shot sent her crashing violently to the forest floor, her arms outstretched, tignon flying, sweat splashing from her ebony skin as she hit the ground. Her peace would come now—sealed by the heartless squeeze of an itchy trigger finger. The sight of Mercy being shot in the back sent the two black men running alongside her diving desperately into the thick undergrowth for cover. Topher and Skibby were a wretched sight, looking as if they had just been to Hell and back then back again for more of the customary punishment dished out there. Their clothes were tattered and soaked with sweat, their nappy hair and Topher's thick beard caked with dirt and debris. They glanced in horror at one another, the devastation they must surely have felt seeing Mercy gunned down like a dog. But no time for mourning in their life-and- death situation. Grief was an unwarranted luxury in this unforgiving wilderness and a distraction that could easily get you killed. Shock and sorrow registered on their faces for an instant before Topher and Skibby scrambled to their feet. Exhausted and on the verge of collapse, they crashed frantically through the dense forest to an uncertain future.

The hard-charging horsemen slowed to an easy trot as they came upon Mercy's lifeless body lying face down in the dirt, a fresh bloodstain in the middle of her back. Smith, his cheek bulging with a giant wad of tobacco, spat a gob indifferently in Mercy's direction, confirming his contempt for the dead nigger to his fellow riders. Boudreaux followed with a disingenuous half-hearted sign of the cross—a remnant of his Catholic upbringing and indication he had long ago abandoned any real Christian beliefs. None of these men showed any signs of devout compassion or remorse, only smirks and cold glares as they passed. The embodiment of callousness, their animosity toward Mercy and their cruel satisfaction in killing her was unsettling. One can only surmise what childhood mistreatment had brought them to this ruthless state of being. Or perhaps it was simply the abuse of their fraudulent power over black people. The posse wasn't overly concerned that Topher and Skibby had eluded them either. Hunting the slaves was sport. The posse knew the two runaways were on the brink of collapse and that it was only a matter of time before the horses rode them down.

Topher and Skibby plowed blindly through the thick forest, uncaring which direction they were headed as long as it meant putting some distance between themselves and the posse. They frantically swatted foliage out of their way as they crashed through the wilderness, desperate to survive, their world rapidly closing in around them. As much as the situation demanded the two men keep running, their bodies were incapable of compliance, the need for oxygen overriding the will to survive. Crippled with fatigue and the posse in hot pursuit, Topher and Skibby did the inevitable … they stopped to catch their breath. It went against every instinctual fiber but there was no alternative. They had nothing left and stopping was a cruel reality. Hidden by the dense undergrowth, they stood bent over, heaving wildly, gulping desperately as their lungs burned, starved for air. Topher was the worse of the two. Barely able to stand and fighting hard to stay upright, he finally fell to his hands and knees. It was clear there was no way he could continue … and with his beloved wife Mercy dead, he had absolutely no desire. Exhausted, desperate, and running out of options, Topher and Skibby looked at one another, both thinking the same thing.

With a slight nod Topher conceded, affirming their silent agreement. "Go on, find yo' freedom," he gasped, his voice raspy with fatigue. Mustering the last of his strength, Topher carefully pulled something from around his neck: a carved wooden figure threaded on a thin leather strap. He looked the ancestral pendant over admiringly, channeling what he could of his ancestors' wisdom and courage, then stuffed the keepsake into Skibby's hand. "Take this with you. At least a part of me can be free," Topher bade, his lungs wheezing as he spoke.

Topher had worn the necklace as far back as he could remember, ever since it was given to him as a young boy by his mother, who had been given it to her as a young girl by her mother. The carved figure had passed

16

through generations, going all the way back to their homelands in Africa. It had a deep, sacred significance and wasn't something either of them took lightly.

Skibby's fist wrapped tightly around the necklace. He looked reassuringly into Topher's eyes as he made his solemn promise. "Don't worry yo'self none, brother. I'll guard it with my life," Skibby assured earnestly, grossly overestimating his ability to carry out such a lofty pledge.

Topher did his best to find a glimmer of hope in their disastrous situation, understanding now that he would probably never see his brother again. "I'll be wantin' that back when I sees you again," he said, his false optimism difficult to veil.

In that moment Skibby also came to realize he would most likely never see Topher again. As the posse closed in on them, they gazed at one another with brotherly affection, savoring every bit of their final moment together. Parting ways was heart wrenching, yet the urgency of the moment demanded they set feelings aside and maintain their presence of mind.

So, without uttering a word Skibby turned hesitantly then charged recklessly into the dense vegetation. The uncharted wilderness quickly swallowed him up, and he was gone.

The excited dogs surrounded Topher, his living nightmare now fully realized. They seemed to take pleasure in terrorizing him, barking and snarling, baring their sharp teeth as if trained specifically to hunt people of his sort. He stood motionless, his arms held close to his body, daring not move lest he give the dogs any more reason to attack. As Topher stood frozen in torment, the posse thundered in and circled him. They glared down from their horses with disdain, savoring their moment of victory and Topher's ultimate defeat. No love was ever lost between Topher and these men, the derision they felt toward each other written plainly on their faces. Yet the bitterness between them lived much deeper, fermented in the cauldrons of time by centuries of white supremacy and the opposing struggle against racial oppression. Defeated, Topher fought to hold back tears of indignation and grief, managing at least to hold his head up, proud and defiant—the only thing he could do to preserve in himself a sense of dignity and worth, wondering what right the posse had to stifle the sovereignty of another human being.

Satisfied with his dogs' performance, LaSalle jammed two grubby fingers inside his pursed lips and blew. The shrill whistle silenced the frothing dogs, some of whom were already pointing eagerly in the direction Skibby had made his escape.

Smith saw fit to spit another indifferent wad of tobacco, this time at Topher. "Look like time done run—"

"Get on with it. Shoot me in the back like ya'll done did Mercy," Topher pleaded, cutting Smith off mid-sentence, uninterested in what any of his captors had to say. Topher had arrived at a mental state in which he no longer cared about the deathly consequences of his own words.

Now LaSalle, being an antagonistic lout and of deranged disposition, didn't take kindly to Topher's insolence … and took the opportunity to set the nigger straight.

"Normally, I'd be against shootin' someone in the back, but when they's a nigger runnin…" LaSalle rasped, fanning the flames of Topher's hidden rage.

Not wanting to miss out on the verbal assault and keen to stay on LaSalle's good side, Smith chimed in. "LaSalle gonna wear you out boy, he don't cut them heel strings first."

Master Jack raised a slight hand, his call for silence. It was clear he was in charge and the posse ceded to Master Jack's authority. "Nigger Topher will set a nice example for any others with a mind to runnin'," he said condescendingly, ignoring Topher's presence. Master Jack was free to speak openly about a lowly nigger, especially a runaway, and the posse shared nods of agreement to his sentiments.

Having secured the group's silence,

Master Jack looked around, gauging the members of his posse, finally singling out Smith and Austin Clay, the youngest member of the posse. Austin couldn't have been much more than twenty, and Master Jack saw fit to spare his only son any further tribulation chasing after Skibby. "Ya'll two get him handled," Master Jack instructed, motioning to Smith and Austin with a nod.

The two appointees begrudgingly maneuvered their horses toward Topher, upset they would miss the upcoming action and excitement of capturing Skibby. Master Jack beckoned the remaining three members of the posse, LaSalle, Boudreaux and Guidry.

"Ya'll come on. Boy can't be far off."

"Naw, he ain't far," Boudreaux exclaimed as he sniffed hard at the hot, muggy air.

"Well then," Master Jack replied

softly, almost to himself, growing weary of the posse's puerile company. They were employees, after all, and Master Jack put up with them largely for the sake of his plantation. He wheeled his horse around in the direction of the pointing dogs then buried his spurs in the horse's flanks, eager to continue the hunt for Skibby. His colt responded with vigor, bolting away in a blur, dirt spraying from its hooves as it sped away.

Not to be outdone, LaSalle, Boudreaux, and Guidry dug their spurs in and thundered off in close pursuit. As they galloped away, LaSalle glanced over his shoulder and let out another shrill whistle, prompting the eager dogs to tear after him.

Austin watched enviously for a moment as

Master Jack and the others sped away then turned his attention back to the matter at hand. He pulled his revolver and trained it on Topher, who was still standing motionless.

As Topher stood stock-still, staring blankly into the distance, Smith slid his burly frame down from his horse and stepped back to the saddlebag hanging from the horse's flank. He untied the leather bag's strap and inserted his pudgy hand, the shackles inside jingling hauntingly as he did—a prelude of things to come.

Smith's tobacco-stained grin flashed tauntingly as he forced the shackles onto Topher's ankles and wrists. Silently enduring the humiliation of being clamped in irons, Topher remained still and lifeless. It wasn't until Smith placed the noose around Topher's neck and cinched it tight that a spark inside Topher finally ignited, visions of past lynchings snapping him from his daze. His flared nostrils and smoldering eyes gave way to fists clinching tightly at this final indignity and the finality of his failed quest for freedom. Topher was going back to whatever nightmare he had escaped from, and he was going back in chains.

Smith pulled at the noose, checking its snugness around Topher's neck, then fastened the other end securely to his saddle. Satisfied, he grabbed the saddle horn, stabbed his foot into the stirrup, and hoisted up his sturdy frame. He swung his heavy leg over to the opposite stirrup and settled in. "C'mon, boy. You got here on two legs, damn sure how you gettin' back," Smith declared as he gave the noose another sharp tug.

On horseback Smith and Austin navigated the terrain effortlessly, easily outpacing Topher who was struggling to keep up, stumbling along at the end of the taut rope, the chains of his leg irons jingling between his ankles. It wasn't long before they came upon Mercy's dead body.

Smith and Austin slowed to a stop, Smith's first order of business being another wad of tobacco spat scornfully in Mercy's direction as he climbed down from his horse. Squatting stiffly, Smith rolled Mercy over, her lifeless eyes staring back at him. She was pretty, even in death, and this time Topher lost the battle holding back his emotions. As bitter tears rolled down his cheeks, his head shook in disbelief—the unbearable sight of Mercy lying there, the life drained from her precious body.

Austin walked his horse up, turning the dark brown bay to face away from Mercy before dismounting. Together, he and Smith reached down and grabbed Mercy by the arms and legs, grunting as they swung her limp body onto the rump of Austin's horse, Topher cringing as he stood by watching. Smith delighted in Topher's anguish, always keen to remind himself that no matter how low his own social status and how dreadful his life, Topher's would always be lower and worse. Austin's heartlessness didn't rise nearly to the level of Smith's, even showing a hint of remorse as they swung Mercy's body up. Despite emulating his father, Austin was still his mother's child and carried a tiny shred of her compassion, although his tinge of regret meant nothing to Topher and wouldn't bring Mercy back. Fighting past his devastation, Topher watched intently, searing the moment into his memory. The posse could easily have left Mercy to the wolves, but like Topher, the sight of her dead body would set a nice example for the other slaves with an inkling to run.

Mercy's body secure, Smith remounted and twisted himself around for a better look at Topher … and another twist of the knife. "Look here, boy. Run again, wind up like your Mercy here."

But Topher wasn't listening. He hadn't heard a single word. His eyes were busy burning a hole through Austin's shirt. "This all yo' fault," he accused Austin flatly, placing whatever blame for Mercy's death squarely with the master's son.

Smith couldn't help but wonder the meaning of Topher's bold accusation, eyeballing Austin suspiciously, eager for more turmoil. Unwilling to acknowledge Smith's questioning gaze, Austin avoided eye contact, focusing his attention somewhere off in the distance.

"Let's get on with it," Austin muttered,

nudging his horse forward.

Not entirely satisfied, Smith relented and turned his attention back to Topher. "Ain't never a good day to be a caught nigger." Topher stared back, cold hatred burning in his eyes.

Master Jack, Boudreaux, Guidry, and LaSalle eased to a slow trot, scanning the undergrowth, searching diligently for any signs of Skibby's passage. As the keen dogs sniffed frenetically, homing in on Skibby's scent, their feverish barks again echoed through the forest.

Hearing the relentless dogs bearing down on him, Skibby quickened his pace, moving as fast as his fatigue would allow. His heart raced as he stumbled along in an exhausted stupor, his thoughts focused on one thing: staying alive. But thoughts alone proved inadequate, and his weariness finally won out. Unable to maintain his balance and overpowered by gravity, Skibby crashed down a small embankment into a shallow ditch, dirt and debris spraying as he landed. Dazed and disoriented, he took a moment to collect himself then gasped in horror at the realization … he'd lost the pendant. He searched the ground around him in a frenzied panic but to no avail. There was nothing to be found. Having wanted a quiet moment to ceremoniously place the keepsake around his neck, Skibby had kept it balled tightly in his fist. The notion of losing the familial necklace moved him to the brink of surrender and almost to tears, but he couldn't give up on finding it. He mustn't. Not now. Not after everything he and Topher had been through. And not after Mercy. What good would freedom be without it? And besides, he had made a promise ... So, fueled by adrenaline, and with the last of his strength, Skibby clawed his way back up the embankment. As his head peeked over the rise, he spotted the necklace lying in the undergrowth—and the posse closing in on him. His heart hammered in his chest as he ducked down in panic and the implications became clear; he would be the one to break the pendant's centuries-old bloodline, failing to fulfill its destiny by passing it to the next generation. The realization was devastating, but the choice was obvious: break his solemn promise to Topher and live to see another day.

The posse was close now, and Master Jack sensed it. The hairs on the back of his neck tingled as the satisfaction of cornering his runaway nigger drew near. He signaled with a raised hand and the posse's pace slowed to a walk. Skibby could hear the triggers click as the posse went guns up, their revolvers drawn and cocked. LaSalle's sharp whistle silenced the dogs and the primordial forest again went eerily silent.

Skibby tried in vain to suppress his hysterical breathing, his mind racing in sheer desperation as he frantically scanned the forest, searching for some way out, hoping for a miracle. As the posse inched closer, Skibby's eye caught a flash of color in the brush. He quickly peeked over the rise, checking the posse's progress. They were practically on top of him now. He turned again and refocused his attention.

3

Skibby's eyes shot wide at the sight of Ghost Bear partially hidden in the brush—an unfamiliar sight and equally unnerving. His heart raced even faster, not sure what to make of this surprising encounter. "Indians" were people Skibby had only ever heard about and never seen … until now.

Ghost Bear was athletic and lean, his skin a deep almond brown tinged with a reddish hue. The Seminole warrior's shoulder-length black hair was enveloped in a sash turban made from strips of calico, a porcupine hair roach sprouting from the top. His patchwork straight shirt hung softly under a scarf and beads. Colorful war paint accentuated his angular features. Ghost Bear stood emotionless, his gaze moving from Skibby, to the posse, then back again as he carefully surveyed the developing situation. It wasn't every day he saw "civilized" intruders in his forest. Caught in a helpless situation and unsure of Ghost Bear's intentions, Skibby's eyes pleaded to the Seminole for help. Trespassers being unwelcome, Ghost Bear answered with a cold stare.

Ten other members of a Seminole war party were scattered throughout the forest. Bona fide warriors, these men were lean, muscular, and battle tested, and today they were armed with bows and arrows, their faces painted for war. Although honed for battle, their vantage point made them unaware of the scene unfolding before Ghost Bear. One of them, Crow Dog, was crouched in a thicket about fifty feet away on Ghost Bear's right flank. The number and color of egret feathers he wore in his headband distinguished Crow Dog as the Seminole war chief. Ghost Bear communicated his findings to Crow Dog with hand signals. *Homme noir ... ten paces ... unarmed ... Qautre cheveux blond ... one hundred paces ... horseback ... armed.* Crow Dog was no-nonsense and a man of few words. He processed the information from Ghost Bear and responded matter-of-factly, or to be more precise, he signaled in a very choppy and deliberate manner for emphasis. *This is not our battle to fight,* he proclaimed. Although vastly superior fighters against the inept intruders, Crow Dog had come to understand the value of restraint. As the posse inched closer and the tension mounted, Ghost Bear took another long, cold look at Skibby, calculating the consequences of his next action.

The flash of color stood out against the green backdrop as Ghost Bear bolted into the clear, extending his sinewy arm to Skibby in a dual act of bravery and mercy.

Surprise quickly turned to excitement as the posse caught sight of Ghost Bear pulling Skibby to safety. Thirsting for action, they spurred their horses and charged in with abandon, dispensing a hail of bullets along the way. Shoot now, ask questions later seemed their credo and today was no reason for them to do otherwise. As the posse bore down, a thick white cloud of gun smoke wafted into the air and lingered, making it difficult for the riders to see what they were shooting at.

A lucky bullet did find its mark, and

Skibby winced in pain as it ripped through his shirt, grazing his right arm, the heat from the hot lead partially cauterizing the small wound it had just created. Amidst a stream of bullets hissing past, Ghost Bear managed to pull Skibby to safety behind a large craggy oak tree.

And with Ghost Bear now on the receiving end of gunfire, his fellow Seminoles maneuvered swiftly to assist. In an instant, a flurry of arrows whizzed toward the posse as war cries echoed through the forest.

In another part of the wilderness, Topher cringed at the sound of gunshots ringing out in the distance. Although born of desperation, what began as a journey of hope and optimism had now come to its tragic conclusion. Smith and Austin paused to listen, then Smith turned to Topher, grinning smugly. "Look like two dead niggers on your hands."

Arrows whizzed in at the posse from three sides. The horses whirled in panic as the posse returned fire haphazardly, shooting blindly through the gun smoke into the trees. As Boudreaux unloaded his revolver at the enemy he couldn't see, an arrow hissed in, piercing him through the heart. The force sent him tumbling backwards head over heels from his horse and crashing to the ground. Moments later an arrow sliced Guidry's carotid artery, spewing a shower of blood everywhere. Guidry's eyes rolled back into his head as he spilled from his horse and slammed into the forest floor, his boot catching in the stirrup as he did. The horse sped away panicked, dragging Guidry along through the dirt and undergrowth. The

Seminoles were surgical in their attack. The posse was no match for the war party and would all soon be dead.

With Skibby safely out of harm's way, Ghost Bear yanked an arrow from the quiver slung across his back and effortlessly nocked it in his gently curved cypress bow. In one fluid motion he spun from the tree, pulled back sharply on the bowstring, and deftly released his fingers. The arrow sprang out, hissing through the air, finding its mark deep in Master Jack's thigh.

The sting from the arrowhead piercing Master Jack's flesh was instantaneous. He recoiled in pain and crashed from his horse, the arrow snapping off in his leg as he hit the ground. His eyes squeezed shut just ahead of his agonizing scream.

Stunned from the violent impact and in imminent danger, Master Jack shook his head, blinking profusely as he hastily tried to regain his bearings. As his eyes came into focus, there, inches from his nose, was the wooden necklace. Master Jack knew exactly what it was and who it belonged to. He snatched it up and stuffed it into his waistcoat pocket before scrambling to his feet and flinging himself recklessly aboard his horse, fear and desperation pumping through his veins. Dangerously overmatched, Master Jack and LaSalle wheeled their horses and dug their spurs in with vigor, neither man bothering to look back as their horses burst away at full gallop. They were alive only because the Seminoles had determined it so— an act of charity and an unspoken warning to the intruders never to return.

The battle now over, exhausted and disoriented, Skibby sat behind the disfigured oak tree, staring blankly at his bloodstained shirtsleeve. Thoughts of the past several days and his unsettled future filled his head. *Too many days runnin' to count. Somewhere out there is freedom ... and now I'm left here to search it out alone. Life is strange. It's funny how quickly things can change.* Skibby's head leaned back against the tree as he slowly drifted out of consciousness.

4

LOUISIANA · JULY · 1853

Bayou Saint Claire was breathtaking in its grandeur. The main plantation dwelling, the *Big House*, sat like a white jewel in the midst of thick green vegetation—a stately mix of Greek Revival, Spanish and French Créole architecture. Nearby was a stable and other outbuildings, a detached kitchen, and to the rear several slave cabins close enough for convenience but far enough to maintain adequate distance between the slaves and their master. The outbuildings were several notches down in splendor from the Big House and the slave shanties even more so. Spanning the entry to the ancient plantation's expansive grounds was a wrought iron archway resting on thick brick pillars, the words *Bayou Saint Claire* spelled out in beautiful black ornate letters. Leading from the gateway to the house was a wide pathway lined with centuries-old oak trees dripping with Spanish moss, creating a natural archway and leading visitors to the house in mystical splendor. A pretense to what took place beyond.

Now in his mid-fifties, John Clay, master of Bayou Saint Claire, had inherited the plantation in 1815 at the age of seventeen—

his mother, father, and only brother having died aboard the paddleboat *Belle Créole* when it caught fire and sank on its return passage from St. Louis. His father and brother had traveled up the Mississippi River to St. Louis to procure new cotton trade deals with the clothing factories there, and his mother had gone because she had never been north of Baton Rouge and fancied a grand adventure. Young Master Jack had requested to stay and look after the plantation, his intention being to establish his own authority in his father's absence. After his family's tragic death and the short period of mourning that followed, Master Jack exerted his influence, quickly putting his own stamp on Bayou Saint Claire. The trade deals his father had made paid off and the plantation flourished under Master Jack's stewardship. Known for the success of Bayou Saint Claire, Master

Jack was additionally well known in the region for his proclivity—some would argue his perversion—to purchase and keep only the prettiest slave girls regardless of their competence at cooking, cleaning, or working the fields picking cotton.

It was picking season at Bayou Saint Claire and field upon field of cotton was in full bloom, a sea of white blossoms stretching as far as the eye could see. Several slaves were busy working the fields, picking cotton in the sweltering afternoon heat. The task was grueling and the slaves hummed as they worked, an effort to occupy their minds with something other than the inhumane treatment and backbreaking labor. Harmonizing held power over their adversity and strengthened their collectiveness. In the fields, each slave carried a canvas sack strapped over the shoulder—the mouth of which was about waist high—where they stored the cotton as they picked.

LaSalle was on horseback at his usual station, at the edge of whatever cotton field the slaves happened to be picking that day, wearing his ever present scowl. He was too busy swatting flies, trying to beat the heat, to pay much attention to the slaves and their goings-on, although his presence was a constant reminder to them of their tenuous, servile existence. Smith was on foot, his dreaded whip in hand, constantly needling the slaves and driving them to work harder. It was a job he relished.

A pair of worn boots lay still amidst the rows of cotton. They belonged to Skibby, who was lying on his back staring blankly up at the sky, a small tattered book resting open, facedown on his chest. A sharp kick to the shin ended his ill-advised daydream.

"Wake up, fool!" Mercy snapped under her breath, just audible enough for Skibby to hear but not loud enough to draw Smith's attention.

"Jesus." Skibby winced, staring up at Mercy's daunting figure silhouetted against the glaring midday sun.

"Rest time over. Time fo' workin," Mercy shot back, annoyed by what she perceived as Skibby's shiftlessness. She hovered over Skibby scornfully a moment longer, damning him with her eyes, then turned her attention back to the endless rows of cotton and resumed picking. Mercy knew from experience that any attention drawn to one slave was unwanted attention for them all. It was the great irony of their situation—that they sought to be seen and treated as human beings, yet their well-being and survival required they spend their days being as unseen and submissive as possible. Not drawing attention to oneself was an invaluable skill.

Skibby sat up and collected himself then rubbed his shin as he contemplated how to further torment Mercy—something he had become very adept at. "Mercy, why you think we here?" he questioned, goading a response and playing with fire.

Mercy had heard the question a thousand times before and was still not amused by it. "We here to pick cotton and not be askin' questions. Somethin' you obviously ain't too familiar with," she replied. "No 'count," she continued under her breath.

To say Skibby and Mercy had a prickly relationship would be an understatement.

They spent a good deal of their time getting on each other's nerves, as in-laws are sometimes prone to do, but Skibby and Mercy had taken their antagonism to new levels. A "no account, good-for-nothing" summed up Skibby perfectly in Mercy's opinion. Skibby shrugged her off as he always did then picked himself up, stuffing the book into the pocket of his warn trousers. It was highly unusual behavior for a slave, in a cotton field, on a plantation—the kind of behavior that usually resulted in painful lashings across the back. But Skibby was peculiar in that way, taking ill-advised chances, toying with the overseers and daring them to catch him out, knowing the punishment he would face. It was a game he played to maintain a sense of aliveness—to experience the thrill of walking up to the precipice of danger and feel the surge of adrenaline as he teetered over the edge looking down into the void, staring peril squarely in the face.

"Nigger Skibby! Get to pickin'!" Smith barked, having taken notice of Skibby and his cavalier attitude toward his picking duties.

The other slaves instinctively picked up their pace, careful not to make eye contact with Smith and give him reason to use the bullwhip he was carrying, knowing the slightest sideways glance could trigger his ire. LaSalle swatted one last fly as he perked up on his horse. He was paying attention now, Skibby and Mercy continuing to bicker as he leered at them from afar.

Now that he had succeeded in drawing Smith's attention and displeasure, Skibby started picking cotton but not with any real earnestness. "Why God set us here anyhow? Bet He ain't never had to pick no cotton," he mused.

Mercy wasted no time responding. "Best get that cotton from between yo' ears," she warned, her head shaking with contempt.

But Skibby hadn't really wanted an answer to his question. "Or feel no whip," he continued.

Always counted on to pick more than his share of cotton, Topher was picking diligently a few rows over when he noticed LaSalle focusing on Mercy and Skibby. Eager to warn them, he slowly made his way over, being especially careful not to draw attention to himself. "Ya'll fixin' to get LaSalle over, ya heard me?" Topher whispered as he approached.

"Not if yo' brother stop talkin' that nonse—"

Mercy stopped speechless, her jaw sagging open. LaSalle was right there on top of them, leering down disdainfully as he gently thumbed the whip resting on his saddle.

"Got my eye on y'all," he hissed.

Mercy and the others quickly averted their eyes—out of fear more so than deference or respect—but they could still sense LaSalle glaring at them menacingly. *This fool crazy!* they all thought.

"Look here," LaSalle demanded, prompting all three slaves to shift their gaze slightly upward at him. They did so warily, never looking him directly in the eyes.

Now that he had their full, undivided attention, LaSalle focused on Mercy, ogling her, wantonly undressing her with his eyes. He wet his lower lip lustfully then watched the slaves for a moment as his obscene gesture hit home. Satisfied his intentions were unmistakably clear, LaSalle pulled his horse around and slowly walked away, basking in his lascivious authority.

All the slaves felt the sting of LaSalle's gesture, but Topher felt it the most. "I be damned," he whispered to himself, shaking his head—ashamed for not taking a stand but helpless to actually do so. The social norms of the era dictated there was nothing he nor anyone could do about what they had just witnessed. Any objections to LaSalle's lewd behavior would bring swift and severe consequences. Smith grinned slyly, delighting in the slaves' humiliation. As he did, they quietly went back to picking cotton, their resentment and outrage festering underneath the surface like a disease.

As the sun sank low in the sky, the clang of

a bell signaled the end of another long "can't see to can't see" workday; sixteen hours of work starting in darkness and ending in darkness. Groups of weary slaves shuffled slowly from the fields in no apparent order and in no particular hurry, their sacks heavy with cotton and for some, LaSalle fresh on their minds. Smith cracked his whip at the slow-moving group—the day's final torment—as they plodded ominously toward the ginhouse: the place where the slaves went at the end of each day to have their cotton weighed before it was ginned; hopeful they had picked enough to avoid punishment. Because Topher usually picked more than was required, he often shared his excess cotton secretly with the other slaves in an act of goodwill and mutual survival. The ginhouse was the most dreaded building on the plantation grounds and loathed by the slaves. On certain days, the distant echo of moans could be heard emanating from its walls, a remnant of past whippings there.

The hot sun and the day's events had taken their physical and emotional toll. Mercy and Skibby left the field together in an unspoken truce while Topher lagged behind, still visibly shaken by LaSalle's lewd gesture … and his own powerlessness to intervene.

As the group made its way to the ginhouse, a wiry slave sauntered up to Skibby. Millie's skin was as dark as night and her clothes hung from her slight frame like a sack on a scarecrow. She nosed so close to Skibby he could smell the blue of her blackness. "Better start doin' some work 'round here," she sassed, her bulbous white eyes exaggerated against her dark skin. Mercy would normally have seized this opportunity to join Millie and take a dig at Skibby, but her mind was elsewhere.

"Ain't nobody ask you nohow," Skibby replied, defensive and embarrassed by Millie's bluntness. Deep down, he knew she was right.

"Don't matter none. Keep it up, you be talkin' to that whip. Smell what I'm cookin'?" Millie continued as she spun around and pranced off thoroughly pleased with herself.

On his way to the ginhouse, Topher crossed paths with the young Master Austin and Celeste, Austin's ten-year-old sister. Bright and energetic, Celeste was still not fully aware of the social constraints of the era.

"Howdy, Mister Topher," she greeted cheerfully.

"Evenin', Miss Celeste," Topher replied, nodding obediently. He avoided direct eye contact, his grip tightening nervously around the strap of his cotton sack.

One of the social constraints of the era was that a black man, especially a slave, not look upon a white woman no matter what her age. Topher continued hurriedly on his way, avoiding any further contact and putting an end to the uncomfortable interaction.

"A bit less cordial with the niggers," Austin scolded his young sister before Topher was out of earshot. Although only twenty, Austin was the eldest child of a slave master, giving him license to do and say whatever he damn well pleased. He had learned well from his father.

"Well, Topher's almost like kin," she replied, looking up to catch Austin's admonishing frown. Although much younger and perhaps because of it, Celeste was more apt to treat the slaves with a modicum of respect. "Aw, don't be so ugly."

But Austin was not to be deterred. He placed his arm around Celeste, a big brother's tough affection. "I promised Mamma I'd never let you come to any harm. I don't intend for you to make me out a liar."

Celeste didn't understand Austin's meaning and thus left it at that.

Topher, Mercy, and Skibby shared a small shack consisting of a small main room and two tiny bedrooms. Built of wood timbers and mud, the ramshackle shanty sat atop foot-high brick pillars to protect it from flooding during the heavy spring rains. The rickety front door hung askew on its loose hinges, causing it to swing slowly open if not latched properly. A narrow covered porch ran the length of the shanty and the interior was plain and sparse, giving an unmistakable sense of the slaves' meager existence. Inside hanging in the small fireplace above a paltry fire was a cast iron pot. A few sundries rested on the open shelves and counters, and a wooden washtub and washboard sat under the only window in the main room of the dwelling. The smell of burning wood and simmering stew wafted through the room.

The three slaves sat around a small rough-hewn table, on top of which a lantern joined with the fire to wash the room in a soft flickering light. They were full—by slave standards—from their evening meal, which this night consisted of corn meal, greens they had planted and harvested themselves, lard, meat, and molasses. The room was unusually quiet, LaSalle's crude gesture fresh on everyone's mind and no one daring mention it. Mercy and Skibby weren't even exchanging their usual verbal jabs and continued their silent truce, Skibby picking at table splinters, Mercy thumbing the small Bible she kept in the lower front pocket of her apron. Mercy finally stood and began clearing the scant bowls and spoons from the table in an attempt to distract herself. Topher and Skibby watched silently as she did.

Topher, being the elder brother to Skibby and husband to Mercy, was in many ways the man of the house and was usually the voice of reason and calm. He took it upon himself to break the awkward silence and take their minds off LaSalle. He did so with the first thing that came to mind. "Hot one today," he said, garnering curious looks from Mercy and Skibby, since it was hot every day during picking season at Bayou Saint Claire.

"Hot one tomorrow too," Skibby replied sarcastically, highlighting the obvious.

The strained silence continued amidst pensive glances … then Topher made another attempt to ease the tension. "Heard me somethin' today."

Skibby and Mercy waited indifferently for the rest of Topher's statement then finally Skibby responded. "Well, go on. You gon' tell us anyhow, ain't you?" he asked, slouching in his chair uninterested, still picking at table splinters.

"Rev say he hear the gov'ment be comin' 'round, recruitin' colored folks," Topher responded.

Skibby quickly sat up in his chair, suddenly interested in what Topher had to say, eager to hear more. The words "recruiting" and "colored folks" meant one thing to Skibby, and his optimism began to percolate.

Mercy on the other hand was not convinced, having never seen black people utilized for anything except slavery. "Colored folks?" she questioned dismissively.

"Need help … killin' some Injuns," Topher explained.

Excited by this news, Skibby jumped at the opportunity to talk about his favorite subject … freedom. "Free pass what that is," he declared. "Get off this here plantation and get free."

Topher realized his mistake in saying anything as soon as Skibby mentioned freedom. He had only wanted to deflect their thoughts away from LaSalle but had instead ignited a fire. And once Skibby got going about freedom, it was difficult to stop him. Skibby had never completely accepted his fate as a slave and freedom was his personal crusade. If not for the repercussions of doing so, he'd gladly spend every waking hour talking about it, believing there was more to life than his wretched existence. Skibby believed as long as black people were perceived as inferior and remained subordinate and servile, they could never reach their full potential and experience what it felt to be fully human.

But Topher knew the attainment of freedom was an impossibility. He made an attempt to douse the flames he'd just ignited and put an end to Skibby's false hopes. "Just talk. Besides, killin' folks ain't Christian."

"Amen. Ain't Christian," Mercy agreed from the washtub, eager as Topher to quell Skibby's aspirations of freedom. But it was too late. Skibby was just getting started and his hopefulness only intensified.

"You wouldn't kill some Injuns? Even it meant bein' free?" he asked, almost pleading. Skibby hadn't really considered the implications of his words and was completely ignorant of the bloody details killing Indians would actually entail.

Topher adjusted himself in his chair, understanding this was not going to be a quick and easy conversation. "Killin' for white folks ain't bein' free."

Mercy, having finished clearing the dishes and not wanting to miss a golden opportunity to malign Skibby, sat back down at the table in preparation for her ensuing insult. "Skibby, what you know 'bout fightin' anyhow? Only thing you good at killin' is my nerves." The truce was over.

Skibby ignored her, it not being an opportune time for a war of words. He had more important things to discuss. "Don't you never want to be more than a cotton pickin' slave?" he inquired of Topher.

Of course, was the answer. But Topher had to weigh the perils of freedom against the certainty of having his family with him on the plantation, as unconscionable a place as it was. Topher had grown accustomed to the peculiar institution out of necessity.

"I got everything I needs right here," Topher assured, glancing lovingly at Mercy.

"So, Lord knows we ain't in no hurry to leave outta here," she added.

Skibby took this opportunity to strike where Mercy was most sensitive, her strong belief in the Lord. "Seem like your God don't be payin' us colored folks no mind."

This was indeed a heartfelt subject for Mercy, and she quickly pulled the small Bible from her apron pocket, as if waiting for the opportune moment to wield it. The Bible's corner was worn where she regularly thumbed it, and without opening it she began reciting a verse from the book's pages from memory. "And that servant, which knew his Lord's will and made not ready …"

Topher knew from experience the longer their discussion dragged on, the less likely it was to lead anywhere worthwhile. Ultimately, nothing would be accomplished except more disagreement and frustration. He lifted his stocky frame from the table, keen to end the night's chatter. "Come on. Massa got some work for us tomorrow."

"Sunday rest day. Ain't that what your Lord say?" Skibby shot back, goading Topher and Mercy and frustrating them even further.

The day had taken its toll, and Topher was visibly worn. "Well, Massa say we workin'," he insisted.

"Well, Massa can come fetch me," Skibby chirped in defiance of both Topher *and* Master Jack.

"I hope he do. Won't be fo' no social visit," Mercy exclaimed as she stood up from the table in a show of solidarity with Topher.

"Go on, and don't make me have to fetch you neither," Topher ordered, officially ending the conversation.

The discussion now over, Skibby pushed back from the table and headed to his room. "Yessa, Cap'n. I be's ready," he said mockingly as he closed the door to his room behind him.

Mercy blew out the lantern as she and Topher headed to their own tiny bedroom.

Moonlight filtered in through the window of Skibby's room, revealing a small chair, a few tattered books scattered about, and a pallet on the floor. Skibby lay shirtless on the pallet, gently rubbing the brand on his upper left arm marking him the property of Bayou

Saint Claire plantation. The letters *B-S-C* enclosed in a circle had formed a keloid scar there. As his fingers gently glided over the deformed skin, Skibby thought back to the day the brand had been seared into his flesh as a young boy. He remembered his hysteria at seeing the red-hot branding iron and how it had required several men to hold him down and keep him still. He remembered the excruciating pain the hot metal had caused. As he stared up at the ceiling, lost in the bitterness of past memories, Skibby's mind shifted and he began wondering about the future. *Freedom ... what could it hold for me? Those closest to me have submitted to their enslavement. They've become blind. We're dying slow here ... but I want to live.*

His exhaustion finally catching up to him, Skibby's eyes slowly closed. Moments later he was sound asleep.

The back porch of the Big House was typical of large plantation homes in the South, stately and airy and large enough to serve as an outdoor living space. Master Jack's family often gathered there after their evening meal as it provided welcome relief from the indoor heat on hot, humid summer evenings. The porch was adorned with various items: a table and benches, assorted wooden chairs and rockers, some potted plants. A wide wooden staircase descended the few feet from the porch down to the ground, and on the already hot morning an ebony brown horse was tied to its railing.

Master Jack, wearing a leisure suit and straw hat, sat in his wooden rocking chair, quietly idling away the time, finding comfort fanning himself with the day's newspaper he read every morning. A few slave men milled about nearby in idle conversation, seemingly waiting for something or someone. No longer at odds, Topher and Skibby made their way up from the slave quarters and mingled in with the other slaves. As the men chatted, speculating on the day's task, the back door swung open and Celeste appeared with a tray of mason jars filled with tea. She approached Master Jack, who gladly took a glass from the tray, smiling proudly as he did.

Without waiting for any sort of approval, Celeste stepped down the porch steps toward the slave men. "Ya'll care for some tea?" she asked cheerfully.

The slave men all nodded, appreciative and respectful—Master Jack's watchful eye made sure of it. The slave men removed their hats as they each took a glass of tea then drank up quickly, grateful for the refreshing drink but mindful of their place. As the interaction required adherence to strict social rules, they were careful not to seem overly casual.

Rev, an elder slave, stepped forward and cleared his throat, his seniority and tenure on the plantation making him the default spokesman. "Much obliged, Miss Celeste. Just like yo' mamma used to make," he commented, prompting the other slaves to nod agreement. Celeste smiled back, a hint of sadness in her eyes.

As the slaves continued milling about, a flat wagon pulled by two sturdy horses approached from the stable, LaSalle and Smith sitting on a bench seat atop it. A slave man rode in back, overseer to an assortment of tree cutting tools: saws, axes, and the like. The wagon rumbled to a stop next to the porch as Austin appeared out the back door wearing a military style slouch hat, his trousers tucked into his black riding boots. The master's son took his nepotistic position of authority quite seriously. Smith spat a wad of tobacco as they waited.

"Finish up now, Celeste," Austin instructed, prompting the slave men to take a few last gulps of tea and place the mason jars back on the tray.

"Here come straw boss," a slave whispered under his breath, a sentiment held by the slaves regarding Austin's position of authority compared to that of his father's.

The other slaves snickered as they

climbed into the wagon, drawing LaSalle's attention. "Say somethin', boy?"

"No suh, boss," the slave replied obediently, raising LaSalle's suspicion and ire even further.

"Then settle the hell down," LaSalle ordered. "I ain't got forever and a day," he declared, glaring back at the slaves. As he turned his attention back to the team of horses, the slave men subtly mocked him behind his back, coming dangerously close to breaking their strict code of conduct.

The back porch was host to an unusual amount of activity that morning, and Mercy's arrival from the slave quarters only added to it. Topher smiled as she neared the porch, her arms full with a basket of folded laundry.

Mercy often spent Sundays washing linens for the Big House down in her shanty, making full use of all available washbasins and satisfying Master Jack's desire for maximum efficiency on the plantation.

Agitated and eager to get underway, LaSalle urged the team of horses with a shout and a yank of the reins, jolting the wagon forward and jostling the slave men in back.

Austin acknowledged his father with a nod before stepping down the porch and untying his horse. He took the reins and hoisted himself aboard as Master Jack peered over his newspaper indifferently. As Mercy passed, she glanced at Austin without feeling or emotion—respectful but apathetic. Austin on the other hand, eyed Mercy wantonly, which did not go unnoticed by Master Jack … or Topher. Seemingly unmoved, Master Jack casually went back to reading his newspaper.

Topher looked as if he'd just taken a punch to the gut. He was quite accustomed and usually numb to white men ogling Mercy. Sometimes they snuck clandestine glances, but most often the looks were unapologetically overt. It was a normal consequence of being a slave and had never amounted to anything more than the indignity and insult of it. But this time was different and Topher felt it. Suddenly, and without cause, white men weren't just glancing at Mercy but leering at her lasciviously, making their lewd intentions clear, which produced in Topher a feeling of uneasiness and foreboding.

Celeste entered the house through the open back door into a small vestibule where Mamé (pronounced mä-MEE), a house slave, was waiting. Mamé, in her mid-forties, had an air of compassion about her. She took the tray of mason jars from Celeste and smiled gently. "Come on, child. Men folk workin' now."

The slave men were hard at work in the south end meadow, chopping up a twisted, toppled oak tree, singing an old corn ditty as they worked—as always, a coping mechanism and a way to take their mind off the physical labor at hand. Austin observed from a distance atop his horse, his mind elsewhere, while Smith and LaSalle stationed themselves amongst the slaves to better oversee their efforts. As it was Sunday the mood was slightly more relaxed, although the slaves remained ever mindful. A lashing for no discernable reason was always a distinct possibility, no matter what mood Smith and LaSalle seemed to be in—and especially since LaSalle was slightly off kilter. As the slaves worked, the air suddenly took on a unique, evocative fragrance as thick storm clouds moved in overhead. As thunder rumbled, Austin took a moment to gaze up and study the darkening sky.

"Look like we gon' get caught behind this rain," Rev mused as he watched the gray clouds tumble in.

The other slaves took pride in Rev's simple wisdom and seemed relieved at the thought of a cooling rain shower. Another round of thunder crackled before the clouds opened up, giving way to a heavy rainfall. The sudden downpour typified the muggy summer afternoons at Bayou Saint Claire—very powerful and usually fairly short. The slave men paused to welcome the rain and the brief respite from the sweltering heat. Ornery and foul as they were, Smith and LaSalle found it within themselves to allow this short break as they too enjoyed the benefits of the cooling rain. In the din of the storm, Austin turned his horse and quietly slipped away, leaving the men to their work. Topher noticed Austin's inconspicuous departure but thought nothing of it.

Mamé stood gazing out the kitchen window at the summer rainstorm, slightly distracted as she washed up the mason jars in a stone basin. Celeste sat with her chin in her palm, watching Mamé curiously as she often did on summer days when not required to be in school. Mamé enjoyed the company, and even though her back was turned, she could still sense Celeste's mood. "What ailin' you, child," Mamé asked with concern, turning to face the young miss.

"I wonder if God's cryin' for someone?"

"I reckon so, Miss. Rain bring some powerful sorrows." Mamé's answer drew an inquisitive look from Celeste, prompting Mamé to pause. "It ain't nothin', child. I'm just an old lady with some tired ol' memories, that's all."

"You remember Mama?" Celeste questioned, already in possession of the answer.

Mamé's resulting smile was tinged with amusement. She'd had this conversation with Celeste more than a few times and it never got old—for either of them. The stories they shared was the closest they came to having something in common.

"Like it was yesterday," Mamé answered reassuringly. "Your mama was a lot like you. Pretty as magnolia in spring and quick as a whip. Wasn't nothin' she wouldn't do for someone. Treated my boys like kin too … even taught mine's to read and write some. Mmm-hmm, good folk."

"Where's their daddy?" Celeste blurted, the question catching Mamé off guard. This wasn't part of their past conversations and a sad expression befell Mamé's face. Celeste had struck a nerve. Mamé turned and resumed gazing out the window at the rain.

Aside from the patter of rain, it was quiet and still in the slave quarters. The downpour had driven everyone inside. A couple of mangy dogs took shelter under a porch as a slave caught out ran for cover into a nearby shack. Just then, Austin appeared atop his horse at the edge of the slave quarters. He glanced around furtively, this being his first foray into the shanties for his intended purpose, then jumped down from his horse, his boots splashing in the mud.

Mercy gazed at the rain through the small

window in the tiny slave dwelling as she scrubbed clothes against the washboard, adrift in thought. As she lost herself staring at the rain, a pair of muddy black riding boots appeared at the open door and quietly stepped inside.

Mercy sensed something and the hairs on her arms and back of her neck bristled, the unexplainable feeling one gets when someone is standing behind watching. It was as if Mercy felt the microscopic breeze as the air shifted in the room. She turned slowly then stumbled backwards.

"You … needs something?" she asked, alarmed.

6

"As smart as you are pretty," the male voice replied flatteringly.

It was highly unusual for Master Jack to be in the slave quarters, let alone inside a slave shack during the day. Legitimate dealings with the slaves customarily took place out in the open. It could be counted on, however, that acts of treachery were carried out behind closed doors.

Mercy was visibly shaken by Master Jack's presence. "Topher and Skibby out on the south end. They due back any minute," she said, her voice cracking as she did her best to conceal her misgivings about the situation.

Master Jack sensed Mercy's distress, having experienced the same trepidatious reaction with other young slave women. "Relax, girl," he said, a shallow effort to put Mercy at ease.

"W—what you doin' back in the quarters, Massa?"

She knew the answer by the wanton look on his face. Master Jack closed the door and took a step closer … prompting Mercy to inch her way back. He took another few steps forward and placed his hat on the table, his boots tracking mud on the rough wood plank floor. Then he spotted a jar of tea on the counter and motioned to it. "How about a nice drink?" he asked, his feeble attempt to distract her.

"Yessa," Mercy responded hesitantly, reluctantly obeying Master Jack's order. Against her better judgement, she turned to prepare a glass of tea, her body stiffening with apprehension as she did.

In an instant Master Jack was behind her, his hands clamping down on the soft smooth skin of Mercy's upper arms, paralyzing her with fear. His hands slid down to her hips, his warm lusting breath on her neck.

"No, Massa," Mercy pleaded, almost inaudibly, barely able to think. Her eyes closed tightly as she braced herself against the violation of her womanhood. After all these years, it was a wonder Mercy had managed to avoid such an assault. And now, finally, the heinousness of being raped by her master was becoming a horrific reality.

Master Jack pulled Mercy close, violently thrusting his hips forward and forcing his genitals up against her backside as he savored her smell. He closed his eyes, lost in sexual desire, transported back in time to other similar encounters. Mercy struggled helplessly against Master Jack's powerful grip as he basked in the sensation of her earthy aroma and her soft skin underneath his fingertips. Unable to overcome Master Jack's primal strength, Mercy's body went limp as he forced her up against the wall and began pulling up her cottonade gown and tugging savagely at her white panties. As Master Jack clumsily groped Mercy, a mangy dog appeared in the doorway left open by the shoddy unlatched door that had slowly swung open. The dog watched curiously for a moment, and then as if it knew something was amiss, let out a series of shrill barks, startling Master Jack. Unnerved, Master Jack unhanded Mercy, glancing out the window to see the downpour had ended. Aware that slaves would be stirring in the quarters soon, he grabbed his hat and rushed through the doorway, away from incrimination.

Rays of sunlight burst through the parting clouds as Master Jack slipped away from Mercy's cabin and headed toward the edge of the slave quarters. At the opposite edge of the slave quarters, Austin stood watching gape mouthed as his father made a clandestine escape.

Mercy hurried to close the door behind him, leaning her shaken body against it. Feeling violated and betrayed, she buried her face in her hands, devastated by the callous brutality she had just endured.

7

Master Jack stood on the back porch enjoying his pipe as dusk descended on Bayou Saint Claire. The slave men were tired but in good spirits, humming softly as the wagon headed back toward the main plantation grounds in the beautiful early evening light. As the wagon approached the house and rumbled to a stop, Master Jack set down his pipe and stepped down the porch steps to administer instruction to Smith and LaSalle. After doing so, he climbed back up the steps and took up his pipe again. LaSalle relayed Master Jack's instructions to the slaves as they piled from the wagon and filtered into the slave quarters.

Daylight having turned to moonlight, Master Jack, Austin, and Celeste gathered in their evening attire in the beautifully furnished parlor. The expansive high-ceilinged room was replete with masterful works of art, exquisite fabrics, and ornately carved furniture imported from Europe. Southern opulence and comfort at its best and a stark contrast to the meager, sparsely furnished shanties in the slave quarters. Having finished their evening meal, the family continued their nightly routine, retiring to the parlor to catch up on the day's goings-on. For Austin and Master Jack, relocating to the parlor also meant an indulgence of alcohol and tobacco.

Master Jack and Celeste quickly took up residence in large, plush lounge chairs hewn from rich dark mahogany and upholstered in fine velvety textured fabric. Too small to fill her chair, Celeste's feet were left dangling over the edge of the seat cushion. Austin stood gazing out the large parlor window, agitated, making little effort to interact with his family—intolerable behavior had his mother been alive. As the parlor was also where guests were entertained and toys strictly forbidden, Celeste made due fiddling with her dress' lace embroidery.

While his children occupied themselves with their individual endeavors, Master Jack savored the taste and aroma from the Calabash pipe he was smoking. "How did my favorite children get on today?"

"We're your only children, Daddy,"

Celeste giggled, amused by her father's silly question.

Master Jack conceded her observation with a smile. "Son?"

"As well as expected," Austin replied, not bothering to turn away from the window to address his father, still chagrined at seeing Master Jack's hasty departure from the slave quarters. Although Austin's feelings toward Mercy were one-sided, he craved her nonetheless. Aware that it was both sinful and immoral to pursue another man's wife, Austin nevertheless had always wanted to experience Mercy in a sexual manner. That was now impossible, Master Jack having laid unwarranted claim to her.

"Good, I've allowed the niggers some idle time tomorrow," Master Jack informed his son.

"Plenty of cotton to harvest. I'm quite

certain it won't pick itself," Austin replied to the window, his agitation growing.

Sensing his son's irritation, Master Jack took a long, slow drag of his pipe. "Indeed not, son, but slaves are like children. They must be coddled at times, in exchange for servility."

Austin turned finally from the window. "Amongst other things," he proffered, a clear reference to Master Jack's earlier venture into the slave quarters.

Acutely aware of Austin's meaning, Master Jack paused, contemplating how to navigate this delicate situation. Then he nodded in agreement. "Amongst other things," Master Jack repeated. "But choose wisely the well from which you drink," he warned. It was Master Jack's own subtle advisement—that Mercy was off limits. Striving to assert himself often times put

Austin at odds with the supreme authority, his father. His ego bruised, Austin went back to gazing out the window, giving him a view of the solitary figure riding on horseback through the plantation gates.

Tending to her nightly duties, Mamé glided through the open French doors that led into the parlor and politely interrupted the conversation, and in doing so changed the subject.

"Excuse me, Massa. Not to bother you none, but there a Major Thomason come to see you," Mamé announced. Contrary to her statement about being a bother, Mamé relished being privy to Master Jack's conversations. She prided herself on being up to date with the Clay family's latest gossip.

"Show him in, then," Master Jack instructed, moving his pipe away from his lips. "We'll have a bit of bourbon now as well."

Mamé affirmed with a nod then disappeared through the wide doorway.

Topher and Skibby piled through the front door of their shanty, roughhousing playfully as they did. Mercy quickly slammed closed the small Bible she'd been reading and discreetly placed it into her apron pocket. She smiled in spite of herself, trying hard to conceal her anguish, which Topher and Skibby were completely oblivious to.

"Massa done give us the afternoon free tomorrow. Headin' to the fishin' hole, " Topher exclaimed, happy about the unusual act of generosity from Master Jack. It would be a welcome departure from a day of picking cotton.

Skibby plopped himself down at the table and finally noticed the pained expression on Mercy's face. "Look like your best friend done died," he commented teasingly.

Before she could respond, Topher noticed the dried boot prints on the floor and duly pointed them out. "Someone come by?" he questioned. Mercy shrugged ignorance to the footprints, convincing no one but herself.

"Look like it. Left a mess too," Skibby quipped. He and Topher waited for an explanation, unaware of Mercy's harsh secret.

The tortured look on her face spoke a thousand words as tears welled up then finally leaked out. Topher looked at his wife with confusion, ignorant to the cause of her distress … until he remembered Austin eyeing Mercy wantonly at the Big House then quietly slipping away from the south end meadow during the short thunderstorm. Topher's heart sank. The wall of denial he had built to convince himself of Mercy's amnesty to their masters' wicked desires had finally come crashing down. Topher couldn't help thinking that in some way he was partially to blame. He had willingly avoided the reality of Mercy's vulnerability. Perhaps he believed her age, or some other unseen reason, had rendered her safe. As he shook his head, his anger welling up in unison with his feelings of helplessness, his own tears began to spill out. He eyed Mercy with sadness and regret, offering his silent apology. He had deduced Austin the culprit and needed no further explanation.

Mamé reappeared at the parlor doors with Major John Thomason, a middle-aged army officer who looked distinguished in his pressed and polished military uniform. Major Thomason was tall and strikingly handsome, his manner reflecting his family's military stock. His father had served as a general before him, and like his father, Major Thomason had graduated from the United States Military Academy at West Point, where he received his commission as a U.S. Army officer. He served dutifully, proudly upholding his family's long military tradition.

"Major Thomason," Mamé announced as the major removed his hat, gloves, and coat with military precision. Mamé took the clothes and quietly left the room.

Master Jack stood and shook hands heartily with his guest, the two being old friends and this being their first encounter after a long hiatus. It was as if they hadn't skipped a beat. "Evening, Major. Make yourself at home."

"Good to see you, Jack. And please, no need for formalities. John will suffice."

Master Jack settled back into his chair and took up his pipe. Major Thomason also took a seat in one of the ornately adorned chairs as he courteously acknowledged Master Jack's children. "My, you two certainly have grown into a fine pair," he greeted, dishing the customary high-society pleasantries.

Celeste thanked the major with a smile, having moved from fiddling with her dress to making up fantastical tales in her head. Austin was still agitated, but not enough to disrespect a houseguest, especially Major Thomason. He nodded his appreciation and thanked the major for the compliment.

"Tobacco?" Master Jack questioned, gesturing with his pipe.

Major Thomason shook his head. "Thank you, but no. At the behest of my wife, I'm currently engaged in an attempt to cut down on my earthly vices."

Mamé returned on cue to the parlor carrying a silver tray, a bottle and three glasses of bourbon, and a glass of milk sitting atop it. She handed a glass of bourbon to Master Jack, who took a slow sip, savoring its oaky, barrel-aged flavor. "And your heavenly vices?" he inquired of Major Thomason.

Major Thomason contemplated the question just long enough not to appear too eager, believing a small indulgence of whisky now and then was good for a soldier's well-being. "I suppose I could be persuaded to indulge this once," he conceded, finding it hard to pass on a fine glass of bourbon.

Mamé proceeded to distribute the remaining drinks, first to Major Thomason and then to Austin, who didn't waste any time guzzling his down. He turned to the window and knocked his drink back in a single gulp, wanting the alcohol to take effect as quickly as possible and have maximum impact. Mamé placed the tray on a nearby credenza, allowing the men to polish off the bottle of bourbon at their leisure. The way Austin had just thrown his drink back, it wouldn't take very long. After setting the glass of milk on an end table next to Celeste, Mamé pulled a small rag doll from her apron pocket. She handed the doll to Celeste with a warm smile, disobeying the house rule of no toys in the parlor.

Master Jack ignored this slight, deciding as master of the house he could overlook the rule anytime he saw fit. It was his prerogative and more importantly it made his daughter happy. In fact, he wasn't even sure how the rule had come about in the first place. "That'll be all for tonight, Mamé," he said, dismissing her from any further duties.

"Yessa," Mamé replied as she left the group to their conversation. Celeste gulped her milk down then quickly switched her attention to the rag doll.

Topher stood silent and dazed as his mind drifted back in time.

Three adolescent slave children, the youngest no more than ten, stood shackled together on the 'box'—a small wooden selling platform—their faces gripped with panic and fear. Several white men jostled for position in front of the box, bidding on the three children as Mercy and Topher watched teary-eyed and helpless a short distance away, the trauma of losing their children tearing at their souls. Suddenly, two white men whisked the children from the platform, eliciting panicked screams. The children cried out for their parents, struggling valiantly as the two men dragged them away, their sale to another plantation and a new master now official. Mercy wailed in despair, lunging desperately for her children as Topher did his best to restrain her, consoling her despite his own grief.

"Topher ... TOPHER!" Mercy shouted, snapping Topher from his cruel recollection back to the harsh reality of the present.

Topher brushed his sleeve across his

face, wiping away his tears, then closed the door and latched it, his sorrow and regret transformed to determination and resolve. Once more he thought of Austin, believing the young master the offender. "He lay a han—"

"Ain't nothin' happen," Mercy lied. "Lord know what next time you and Skibby out," she speculated nervously. Topher breathed a short sigh of relief but was now faced with the reality of what he had been in denial about for so long: an assault on Mercy was inevitable and only a matter of time.

Skibby understood now too, as evidenced by the *a-ha* look on his face. As much as he and Mercy had been at odds in the past, now was the time to set aside their differences and come together. And now that the stakes were clear, a heightened sense of urgency permeated the room.

"Won't be no next time," Topher declared, rubbing the ancestral necklace through his shirt. Skibby's eyebrows raised. He eyed Topher curiously, uncertain of his brother's meaning. "Mercy ain't safe no more ... ain't got no choice, 'cept runnin'," Topher explained, seemingly relieved by his decision.

Skibby was more than surprised to hear this. In fact, he wasn't really sure he had heard it at all. "Say again?"

"Mercy ain't safe," Topher answered.

"The other part," Skibby replied, taking a deep anticipatory breath.

Topher took a moment to reflect on what he was about to say. He looked at Skibby, determined and assured. "We runnin'," he declared.

Bam! Skibby's fist pounded on the table in triumph. It was a moment he had dreamed of and a long time coming—agreement from his older brother finally to make their escape and in doing so to live free.

Mercy cringed. She picked up the broom and began sweeping anxiously, overwhelmed by this rapidly developing situation. "Lord have mercy."

"I already done lost my children. Ain't gon' lose my wife too," Topher proclaimed.

As Mercy went through the motions of sweeping, Topher informed Skibby he wasn't obligated to join their escape. "You ain't obliged." The events of the day were Topher's cross to bear, and he alone would set things right. It was a virtuous attempt but one that failed miserably.

"Ya'll go ahead on. I'll stick around here slavin' for ol' Mister Charlie," Skibby responded sarcastically, making clear there was no way he would ever miss out on a chance at freedom. After all, it had been his crusade all along.

Topher accepted Skibby's obvious choice with a chuckle. "Come on if you comin', then. But we be just another bunch o' runaway niggas to 'em now," he warned, uncertainty and doubt creeping into his voice.

"Always was. Runnin' got nothin' to do with it," Skibby replied.

"Be sure about it, Massa gon' put LaSalle after us."

The name LaSalle sent a shiver down Mercy's spine. "That dog'd kill ya soon as look at ya," she said, taking a break from mindlessly pushing dirt around the floor.

Topher's mind raced. He sat down at the table, an effort to collect his thoughts and sort through the doubt and chaos clouding his mind and hopefully come up with some semblance of a plan. Skibby and Mercy watched silently while he did, their minds working just as hard to process everything and come to terms with the thought of running away. As his hands wrung together anxiously, Topher's hope that some divine wisdom would come to him slowly faded. Finally, he declared with much uncertainty that it best they make their escape right away as soon as a few provisions could be gathered. Topher was improvising, and his declaration seemed more an effort to convince himself.

Skibby nodded agreement, an attempt to buoy Topher and restore his courage to run. "Put us up the road a piece, 'fore anyone notice we gone. Guess you ain't makin' that trip to the fishin' hole," Skibby added, providing some unintentional levity to the situation.

"Reckon not," Topher conceded.

"What about yo' mamma?" Mercy blurted, adding yet another layer of uncertainty to their hastily laid plans. "She could come with us."

"Mamé don't need to know nothin'. Best she stay here anyhow. Be safer that way," Topher assured Mercy, unsure of any truth to his words. It was more an excuse to avoid telling Mamé and thus avoid her judgement. Informing his mother would be more terrifying than running itself.

The idea of keeping Mamé in the dark did not sit well with Mercy or Skibby and brought frowns to their faces. Skibby's eyebrow raised again as he gave Topher a sideways glance, a subtle appeal to his brother … and a battle Skibby knew he couldn't win.

Without warning, a knock rattled the shanty's front door. Everyone inside stopped motionless as they exchanged concerned glances, wondering if their conversation had been overhead. Another knock followed, this time louder and more persistent.

Topher stood up and approached the door as everyone wondered who could be pounding on it at such a late hour. "Who dis?" he questioned softly, leaning in close in anticipation of the late-night visitor's response.

"Y'all open up. I ain't got all night to be standin' out here," Mamé answered impatiently.

The formalities over and Major Thomason having settled into the evening, Master Jack inquired if the major had any thoughts on the evening's topic. "We were just discussing the merits of tolerance … in trade for servility. Any thoughts on the matter?"

"I can't say that I have any," Major

Thomason responded.

"There must be something you can tender, being an officer of men," Master Jack probed.

"Well, I wouldn't presume to be an authority on the particulars of a cotton plantation," retorted Major Thomason, avoiding the topic, eager to get to the real intentions of his visit.

"Yet I suspect your visit might have some bearing on this plantation, in particular," Master Jack countered.

Major Thomason affirmed Master Jack's suspicions with a nod then quickly took the opportunity to talk about what he had really come for. He stood and began moving about the room, slowly sipping his bourbon. "Jack, I'm sure you're aware of the Indian Removal Act," he stated.

Master Jack affirmed that he had. "I

am. Hell, John, that was signed by Jackson damn near twenty years ago."

"Twenty-three, to be exact," the major corrected. "Then I presume you're aware it requires that all Indians relocate to designated lands west of the Mississippi." Master Jack sucked on his pipe as he nodded, prompting Major Thomason to continue. "The army's job ... my job has been to insure these belligerents comply. Unfortunately, the Seminole Indians in Florida have doggedly refused to heed the order. These natives might have received some clemency if not for the large number of runaway niggers amongst them."

His interest piqued, Austin's attention shifted from what lay beyond the parlor window to the current conversation. Major Thomason stopped pacing briefly to admire a picture on the wall—an image of the paddleboat *Belle Créole* steaming down the Mississippi River. "These so called Black Indians stand to lose their unlawful freedom and have thus shown to be quite determined," Major Thomason continued.

Master Jack digested the information patiently as he took a short drag on his pipe. "If I know anything of Young Hickory," he interjected—*Young Hickory* being the nickname of then current President Franklin Pierce due to his admiration of *Old Hickory*, former President Andrew Jackson (a man who bore a bitter, racist animosity toward blacks and committed brutal genocide against indigenous Americans).

"Yes, Young Hickory indeed," Major Thomason mused before finally getting to the crux of his visit. "Consequently, I'm here to seek out any available slave men to help quell this rebellion. These niggers might finally be of some use," Major Thomason continued, conveniently forgetting who had actually built America and whose land it was built upon.

This time Master Jack took a long extended toke on his pipe then let out a slow billowy stream of smoke in advance of his question. "And once their purpose is served?"

Major Thomason paused, anticipating the negative reaction he perceived was sure to follow. "They'll be granted their freedom." His perceptions were correct.

This revelation did not sit well with Master Jack or Austin, and both sighed in frustration upon hearing the news. Austin, who had been quietly holding his tongue, made clear his unbiased opinion. "Allowing niggers to go free will undermine our entire way of life. And free niggers amount to free enemies."

With no more pictures to examine, Major Thomason took up the seat he had occupied earlier. It was clear his request—that Bayou Saint Claire relinquish slaves to the army's cause—would not be an easy sell. "The allegiances being formed by these savages and fugitive niggers is distressing to our leaders in Washington. Freeing a few slaves is a small price to pay for the ruination of such a dangerous alliance," Major Thomason explained, a hint of desperation in his voice.

Ignorant of slaves' and natives' tribal nature and similarities of culture, and not quite understanding their alliance, a confounded look crossed Austin's face.

"Kindred spirits. A mutual predilection toward savagery and ignorance," Major Thomason explained, understanding Austin's confused expression.

Master Jack had an explanation of his own. "Relinquishing our property to freedom flies in the face of our history."

Understanding their concerns, Major Thomason was still quite determined to make his case. So much depended on it. "We mustn't lose sight here, Jack," he implored. "Rest assured, the benefits will far outweigh the sacrifice."

Master Jack contemplated the proposition then took another long toke of his pipe.

Topher put a finger to his lips, calling for secrecy about their plans. He took a deep breath, feigned a smile, and opened the door. Mamé smiled back warmly as she stepped inside. As she sat down at the small table,

Topher poked his head out the door and looked around suspiciously. Plans like theirs often found a way into the wrong hands. He was not surprised to see Millie leaning idly against a nearby tree. He squinted untrustingly at her then slammed the door shut and latched it.

Mamé settled into her chair, the weight off her feet a welcome relief. "How y'all doin'?" she asked, the tension heightening from her sudden appearance.

"We alright. What you doin' out so late?" Topher asked nervously, his paranoia plain for anyone paying attention to see.

"I got a right to visit ain't I? Just makin' sure ya'll stayin' outta trouble." Mamé's choice of words drew furtive glances from the soon-to-be runaways. "Besides, Massa let me off. He up there sippin' bourbon with the army," she continued, slipping her shoes off to rub her tired feet.

"Come to recruit colored folks," Skibby suggested.

"Just white folk gossip," Mamé assured. That's mostly what the conversations Mamé overheard amounted to up at the Big House: a corrupt politician, a new slave purchase, a neighbor's travels. So Mamé had no reason to believe Major Thomason's visit was anything more significant.

Under normal circumstances, Mamé would have been a calming presence. The night being anything but normal, she was having the opposite effect, causing everyone a great deal of anxiety and stress. Fidgeting anxiously, Mercy finally succumbed to the strain of the evening, defying Topher and his call for secrecy. "Topher got somethin' to say!" she blurted, her pronouncement catching everyone, especially Topher by surprise.

But Mamé had already ascertained the group was up to something based on their unusual behavior. She inquired further. "What is it, son?"

"Huh, ain't nothin'," Topher answered, feigning ignorance as he shot Mercy a subtle look of disapproval.

"Go on, speak up," Skibby goaded, drawing a scowl from Mamé. He quickly sank under the weight of her authority, slouching lower in his chair like a contrite child.

Mamé looked to Topher for a more suitable answer, and Topher quickly averted his eyes to avoid her discerning gaze. "This oughta be good," she said under her breath, anticipating Topher's upcoming lie.

But Topher knew Mamé was too clever and by virtue of being his mother would quickly see past his deception. So instead, he mustered his courage and did the only thing possible given the situation. He told her the truth. "We … We leavin' out tonight."

Mamé's heart sank, though she did her best to conceal it. She had figured something was amiss, but this was not at all what she had expected. "Mmph, mmph, mmph," she sighed. "Look like the rain done brought another dark cloud."

Seeing Mamé's reaction was difficult, especially since the runaways knew they were only moments away from leaving her behind.

"Come with us," Skibby implored, finding himself unwilling to abandon his mother. If anyone deserved to be free, it was her.

Mamé entertained the thought—to finally be liberated from the plantation she had known all her life and live in freedom. The proposition was hard to turn down.

But realizing the implausibility of it, she contradicted her own self-interest and decided against it. "I been on this plantation a long time. Too long to leave now and start changin' my ways," she explained. "I may never see the sight of freedom ... but Mamé gon' be just fine." She turned her attention to Mercy, who clearly was not having an easy time of it. "What about it, Mercy, you gon' be alright?"

No, Mercy was not going to be all right. She had seen firsthand the consequences of failure, and the horrific visions of lynched slaves hanging from tree branches haunted her thoughts. "Wh-what if we caught?" she stuttered, forcing the others to confront the very real possibility and sinking the mood in the room even further.

Mamé, understanding the value of hope, responded to Mercy's question as optimistically as possible. "Freedom not always free," she said. "But you gotta trust what you doin' is right. And don't never stop 'til you find what it is you lookin' for."

"This all hard to believe," Topher reflected sadly.

"No, son, it ain't," Mamé assured him.

Quiet suddenly befell the room as the overwhelming nature of the situation weighed on everyone. And then, just like that, Mamé stood up from the table and made her way toward the door. "Well, that be that. Now let me be gettin' back," she said, trying her best to put up a strong façade and make it out without breaking down in tears.

As Mamé neared the door, Mercy grabbed her and hugged her tighter than she ever had, the sadness of saying goodbye welling up in both of them and moving Mercy to tears. In leaving Mamé, Mercy would be leaving behind the woman who had looked after her when she came to Bayou Saint Claire as a young girl. Mamé had sheltered Mercy, raising her up as her own. Topher and Skibby joined the embrace now, and Mamé hugged the three of them back all at once.

Finally, Mamé managed to pull away and reach the door, stopping to face her children one last time. "Remember, in all thy ways acknowledge Him ..."

And in unison, Topher, Skibby, and Mercy finished her sentence. "... and He shall direct thy path."

Mamé unlatched the door and stepped out onto the porch, leaving the door hanging open. As she stepped down the porch steps, tears finally spilling out, she implored softly, "Lord, deliver my children." Overwhelmed with heartache, her gaze moved to the slow stream of smoke billowing from the chimney of a nearby shanty.

A slow stream of smoke from Master Jack's pipe filtered into the air. "I'll see through to help your cause," he informed Major Thomason. *Topher and Skibby,* he thought to himself.

Austin had seen and heard enough. Relinquishing slaves to freedom went against everything he trusted and believed in, and he would not be party to it. "Come on, Celeste, it's late," he said, angry resignation in his voice. He woke his sister who had fallen asleep slouched in her chair and was now breathing slow, deep breaths, clutching her rag doll. Her heavy eyelids struggled open as she fought off her drowsiness.

"G'night, Daddy," she muttered

sleepily. Austin guided her out of the parlor to her bedroom as Master Jack and Major Thomason nodded back their goodnights.

"A sensible decision, Jack," Major Thomason assured, relieved at having procured something for his cause.

"Perhaps. Time will tell," Master Jack replied, unsure how his decision would impact the future. What he did know was that Andrew Jackson and Franklin Pierce were staunch champions of slavery. If those men, whom Master Jack held in the highest regard, believed pitting slaves against the rebellious Seminoles was in the best interest of the country, and ultimately the slave-holding ideology of the South, well then, he could get behind their cause.

Major Thomason retrieved a small logbook and pencil from his waistcoat pocket, turned to a specific page, and jotted a few notes. "How does two thousand dollars sound?"

"It sounds like we have a deal."

The two men stood and sealed their gentlemen's agreement with a handshake.

"Your sacrifice won't go unnoticed," exclaimed the major. "I'll have my men deliver payment tomorrow. I trust you'll have your bucks ready?"

"I'll see to it they are."

8

LaSalle's living quarters were small and sparse, not much different from a slave's. A few simple furnishings adorned his room and a half-empty bottle of whisky sat on a chair next to the bed. Drinking heavily each night helped LaSalle reconcile his loathsome existence—slightly better than a slave's and due only to the fact that his ancestors had come from Déville-lès-Rouen and not Ndimba.

Asleep on his back, the first hint of

daylight crept in through a small window and settled on LaSalle's face, which seemed tormented by a bad dream. He sprang up, gasping, suddenly wide-awake, sensing something was wrong on the plantation, which prompted him to leap out of bed and scramble for his britches. As he stumbled toward the door pulling up his worn trousers, a set of wiry black toes poked out from underneath the covers.

The three runaways were well on their way to freedom, Topher leading the way, Skibby in back, and Mercy wedged safely in between. They kept low as they ran, skirting the edge of a cotton field that bordered a large forest, nervously scanning for any signs of danger.

Without warning, Topher stopped

abruptly, causing Mercy and Skibby to pile into him just as a wagon rumbled by with two men sitting atop it. The black driver turned, catching sight of the three runaways standing frozen in the waist high cotton, breathing hard, wet with sweat and completely exposed. Not a full day into their escape and the trio had already been exposed.

Not believing his own eyes, the wagon driver looked again to confirm what he had just seen—and by doing so alerted the white passenger, who turned to see for himself. But there was nothing there. The three runaways had vanished.

"What is it, boy?"

"Ain't nuthin', Massa," lied the driver.

Not convinced, the passenger turned again to look then glared doubtfully at the driver. As the wagon rolled into the distance and out of sight, the runaways cautiously picked themselves up in the tall cotton, Skibby deciding it a good time to speak. "Jesus, we damn—"

"Ain't no time fo' preachin'. Run, fool," Mercy interrupted as she clapped Skibby sharply in the back. The three runaways sprinted across the dirt wagon tracks and disappeared into the woods on the far side, having narrowly escaped their first dangerous encounter as runaway slaves.

The narrow game trail snaked its way through the forest for what seemed to the runaways like a hundred miles. The tall pine trees and the changing terrain indicated they were putting some distance between themselves and the bayou plantation they had escaped from the night before. As they clumsily navigated their way through the trees, a fork in the trail caused them to stop abruptly and forced a decision to be made. It also provided a much needed rest.

As the runaways glanced back and forth at the two paths, one leading up a craggy hill and the other continuing down a gentle slope, they contemplated the best option, wondering perhaps which path their pursuers would expect them to take.

Mercy spoke first, as usual reciting a Bible verse to correspond with their situation. "But for those who are righteous, the way is not steep and rough."

Topher and Skibby nodded acceptance, happy the decision in which path to take had been made for them. The trio quickly headed down the gently sloping trail and disappeared deeper into the forest. After several more miles running clumsily along the trail, pushing themselves to exhaustion, they spilled into a small clearing.

Skibby glanced back up the trail,

looking for any signs they'd been pursued by LaSalle or otherwise. Seeing no one, he breathed a sigh of relief. "We made it. We's free."

"Maybe they just ain't caught up," Mercy responded sharply, getting back to her usual self.

"Or maybe we's free," Skibby repeated as he glared back dismissively.

9

LOUISIANA · AUGUST · 1853

The remainder of the posse—Master Jack, Austin, Smith, and LaSalle—rode slowly through the gates of Bayou Saint Claire, worn from their long journey home. Topher stumbled behind, barely able to keep up, exhausted from days of traveling on foot, his ankles rubbed raw from the leg irons he was burdened with. Only a few dogs trotted alongside, thick with dirt and dust.

It was Saturday, and slaves picking cotton noticed from the fields. They stopped their work and watched with stares of disappointment, understanding the ramifications of Topher's failure, knowing he would be administered the harshest punishment.

Seeing the riders returning, three young slave boys took up chase alongside what was left of the posse. Their playfulness waned at the sight of Topher in chains and a noose around his neck … and Mercy's dead body slumped over Austin's horse.

The posse came to a stop at the stable and dismounted as the slave boys somberly tended the horses in silence, not daring uttering a word. Topher instinctively moved toward Mercy, bitter sorrow evident on his face, only to be yanked back suddenly by the noose around his neck. On the other end of the rope was Smith, pulling Topher like a farm animal toward the penal box—an on-site prison cell fashioned from a railway freight car and bereft of any windows or ventilation. It took all of Topher's willpower not to retaliate, which would surely have resulted in his own cruel death.

Tired, longing for the comforts of home and eager for his wound to be tended to, Master Jack limped in pain toward the Big House, helped along attentively by Austin. LaSalle followed dutifully a few yards behind, his intentions unclear.

Having seen the posse's return from the kitchen window, Mamé stood paralyzed, shock having overtaken her body. The porcelain dish she was holding dropped from her hand and smashed into pieces against the stone wash basin, snapping Mamé from her daze. She rushed hysterically out the back door toward the penal box, wailing as she went. "My children. What you done to my babies?" she screamed.

As she rushed pass, Master Jack grabbed Mamé's arm as he tried to quell her hysteria. "Now calm down and get ahold of yourself," he admonished.

But Mamé was overwrought and no amount of reprimand could calm her. She struggled free of Master Jack's grasp, but in doing so stumbled to the ground, right at the feet of the dreaded LaSalle. Master Jack shook his head in frustration as he turned away and continued toward the Big House.

As Mamé lay sprawled on the ground, LaSalle scowled down at her. "Yourn others got what was comin'. Nigger Topher get his tomorrow." Hearing LaSalle's words and overcome with grief, Mamé began sobbing uncontrollably.

At the penal box, Smith sent Topher tumbling to the floor with a violent shove. He yanked the iron door closed then locked it with a large metal padlock. As Topher lay collapsed in the corner, he struggled to loosen the noose around his neck. Unsuccessful, he lowered his head between his knees, overcome, and began to sob

Tied to the whipping post—a high wooden beam supported by two wooden posts— Topher had had a full night in the box to reflect on the failed escape, Mercy's death, Skibby's fate, and the punishment that now awaited him. His hands were bound above his head to the cross beam with a leather strap, his tattered shirt pulled down revealing a back surprisingly free of scars. Several slaves had gathered nearby, Millie and Rev amongst them. The slaves had witnessed this scene play out untold times and had come to provide Topher moral support and psychological strength. They were there to encourage in him the resolve and mental fortitude he would need to make it through his cruel punishment.

LaSalle stood next to Topher, whip in hand, as Master Jack leaned on his new cane, watching intently from the back porch.

As things unfolded at the whipping post, Mamé pled to Master Jack submissively from the doorway, doing her best to save Topher from his upcoming penance, unable to bear the thought of his pain and suffering. "Please, Massa. Topher a good boy. He ain't never been no trouble."

"Topher has seen his share of tolerance," Master Jack answered flatly, not turning to acknowledge Mamé.

"He ain't gon' cause no mo' trouble. I promise he ain't."

"LaSalle's whip should see to it," Master Jack replied coldly.

"But, Massa, he my boy and—"

"Enough!" Master Jack snapped, cutting Mamé off sharply as he turned toward her to drive his point home. "His disobedience will not go unpunished."

Defeated, Mamé turned away, unable to witness her son's punishment.

LaSalle admired Topher's unblemished back, running his rough fingertips across Topher's smooth dark skin. He would enjoy leaving his mark and leaned in to Topher's ear. "First time, huh, boy? Run again, you'll feel more than just my whip 'cross your back," he whispered. Topher's jaw clinched in defiance, in preparation for what was to come.

After ambling to his station about ten feet behind Topher, LaSalle turned to the gathered slaves. "Y'all listen here. Let this be a lesson. Run from me and you got but two choices." He drew his Colt Walker and admired it for a moment then slid the gun back into its holster. "If you smart like nigger Topher here, you'll settle for my whip," he continued as he cracked the whip ominously, making plain his skill at using it. He glanced to Master Jack for the signal to proceed, Master Jack acknowledging with an ever so slight nod.

As he hurled the whip back, LaSalle again glared directly at the gathered slaves, pausing a moment before turning to face Topher and snapping the whip forward. The woven leather strap whistled through the air before it cracked sickeningly across Topher's back, splitting his unblemished skin. Topher was wholly unprepared for the brutal sting and his jaw clinched tighter as he winced in pain. He did all he could not to cry out in agony, a single tear welling up and sliding down his cheek.

The whip cracked again and again as LaSalle meted out lash after lash. The onlooking slaves could hardly watch, feeling each stroke as if it were their own backs being flayed. But Topher made not a sound during his beating. His unwillingness to wail out in pain was setting a bad example for the slaves, something LaSalle could not let go unheeded. He redoubled his efforts and administered a few more punishing lashes, the vibration of the whip reverberating up his arm as sweat dripped from his forehead. Finally, Topher began losing his battle to remain silent and dignified, his legs buckling as he let out a guttural moan with each additional malicious, skin-splitting, stroke. He was close to passing out from the pain as LaSalle continued … Forty strokes … forty-one.

Master Jack seemed moved—more than would be expected—watching a slave being disciplined with a whip, something he had seen hundreds of times. "That's enough," he instructed, having seen his fill of Topher's punishment.

Pretending not to hear, LaSalle hurled the whip back and delivered a final spiteful stroke.

"Enough!" ordered Master Jack, this time shouting to be heard.

Topher was barely conscious now, hardly able to stand, the leather strap securing his hands to the cross beam—the only thing holding him upright.

Satisfied, LaSalle wiped the sweat

from his brow with his sleeve and grinned as he turned again to the gathered slaves. "Y'all niggers go on and git. Remember this here next time you itchin' to run."

The slaves dispersed, quietly seething underneath, careful not to show any emotion.

"Fool got what was comin' you ask me," cracked Millie.

"Well now, ain't nobody askin' you," Rev answered, prompting her to prance off in a huff.

Several hours had passed since the whipping and Topher was still strung up, barely conscious, his head drooping low and his back in tatters. The flies buzzing around his open wounds didn't seem to faze him; the crunch of footsteps approaching did. Topher lifted his head up slowly to see Master Jack limping with a cane toward him.

Upon arrival, Master Jack shifted back and forth on his cane, agitated, shaking his head as he gave Topher a long, hard look. "Am I not a good master?" he questioned.

Topher stared back coldly, his eyes bloodshot from his agonizing punishment, his state of mind altered.

"And this is how you repay my tolerance. By God I will not have a slew of niggers coming and going at will," Master Jack continued.

Topher wasn't listening. He hadn't heard a single word. "Where Skibby at?" he muttered in a low guttural voice.

"Dammit, boy! Skibby is dead," Master Jack hissed, incensed, barely able to contain his anger. "You have those red savages to thank."

Topher was unfazed and continued speaking out of turn, pushing the boundaries of acceptable behavior. He had once again reached the point of not caring about the consequences of his words, as if wanting to die. "You a lie," he said, leaning into Master Jack's face for effect.

Well, this insolence from Topher was just about all Master Jack could handle, the blood vessels in his face filling, turning him an even brighter shade of red. Seething with rage, Master Jack remembered … "A disbeliever," he said as he pulled the carved wooden necklace from his waistcoat pocket. "How about now?" he asked, dangling the pendant in front of Topher.

The sight of his necklace and the thought of it in Master Jack's hands drove Topher to hysteria. He lunged maniacally at Master Jack, the leather bindings squeaking with strain as they kept Topher at bay. Master Jack flinched then quickly regained his composure, remembering he was in the position of authority.

"You see, them Indians are your real enemy," Master Jack persuaded as he cautiously placed the necklace around Topher's neck. He had Topher's attention now. "Shame y'all decided to run. A few more days and you'd have been fightin' against those savages. Maybe even get your freedom."

Topher's body relaxed and his demeanor calmed as he took a moment to let Master Jack's words sink in. "I'll fight your Injuns."

Master Jack balanced himself on his cane. "Act right, boy, you might get your chance." Then he turned and slowly limped away.

LaSalle, who had been doing

busywork within earshot approached Topher quietly. Leaning close, he whispered in Topher's ear. "Over my dead body."

10

Skibby was lying barely conscious in the chikee as a small fire flickered next to him. He opened his eyes slowly and for the second time that day witnessed something completely unfamiliar. Running Dove, a young Seminole woman carefully mended the wound on his arm. She did so with considerable skill and equal detachment. Skibby gazed at her curiously through his half-open eyelids then drifted out of consciousness.

As the warm sunlight kissed his face, Skibby awoke, stiff and sore, to unfamiliar surroundings, the suffocating heat first to get his attention, his unrelenting thirst second. He realized his right shirtsleeve had been cut away, the wound on his arm mended, and tried to remember how. After gingerly pushing himself up from the floor, he massaged the hunger pangs he'd just noticed jabbing him in the stomach then took a look around.

The Seminole village was a primitive new world alive with activity. Several chikees were scattered throughout the village, drying plants, animal skins, baskets, and other goods hanging from their eaves.

As Skibby stepped down watchfully from the elevated platform, he noticed Seminole men and women going about their business, speaking in their native language, paying little attention to their new inhabitant. They were too busy with the task at hand: surviving in the harsh Florida wilderness. The village was unlike anything Skibby had ever seen, and he was surprised to see black men and women there wearing colorful Seminole clothing.

As Skibby stepped from the chikee onto solid ground, he noticed a vessel full of water. Wasting no time, he eagerly cupped several mouthfuls with his hands, quenching his searing thirst. Then he made his way over to a thicket of underbrush at the edge of the village, all the while soaking in his new surroundings. Glancing around to make sure no one had taken notice, he opened the flap on his trousers and began to urinate, sighing with relief as he did.

Just as Skibby began relieving himself, Silas, a sinewy middle-aged black man in Seminole clothing approached, offering his hand to shake. "How do, son? Name Silas."

Alarmed, Skibby flinched, embarrassed by the stranger interrupting his sacred morning ritual, although the apprehension about his unfamiliar surroundings lessened with a greeting from another black man. Silas immediately realized his mistake and sheepishly withdrew his hand, focusing his attention elsewhere in the dense forest. Finally, Skibby finished urinating and took another curious look around, wondering exactly where on earth he was.

"You's in a Seminole Injun camp," Silas informed him, understanding Skibby's silent question.

"Not for long I ain't," Skibby responded, glancing sideways as he closely examined Silas' odd clothing.

"You got a name?"

"Skibby," he said, nodding.

This time Silas examined Skibby from head to toe. Unimpressed, he gazed out at the enveloping wilderness. "Skibby, only thing out there for you is hard times and death."

Skibby followed Silas' gaze into the surrounding jungle then looked scornfully at the Seminoles in the village. Silas understood Skibby's misgivings about this strange new world and its people. After all, he had been in similar circumstances some years ago. "No different from us. We stick together, we all keep free," Silas explained.

But scratching out a living in the harsh wilderness was not the freedom Skibby had pictured so often in his dreams. "Don't unsettle yourself none," he advised Silas. Skibby had no intention of staying.

"Well, before you get to leavin', you hungry?"

Skibby felt his empty belly. "Famished," he exclaimed, prompting a raised eyebrow and a look of confusion from Silas.

Silas was surprised to hear Skibby use such a word. "What you is, educated or somethin'? What that mean anyhow?" Silas questioned.

"Means I could do with somethin' to eat," Skibby explained.

"Ain't no need for them big words around ol' Silas. Never had no schoolin' see."

Skibby was hardly surprised, but the hunger pangs stabbing him relentlessly in the gut kept him from making a snide comment like the ones he so often made to Mercy. Plus, it would have been rude to insult the person that was about to feed him. He hadn't eaten in days and the fact that he had no intention of staying in the Seminole village didn't deter him from a long overdue meal before he went.

Understanding now, Silas made his way through the village, Skibby following eagerly as they wound their way through the chikees. The sight of the villagers' rugged existence only reinforced Skibby's decision to leave. They arrived finally at a communal stew pot hanging over a small fire. The few women cooking and tending the fire greeted Silas, paying Skibby little mind. Silas filled a bowl with sofkee and handed it to Skibby then spooned a bowlful of his own and took a large satisfying gulp. Skibby sniffed skeptically at the mush in his bowl and winced at the pungent, unfamiliar smell. His face contorted as he forced down a mouthful of the unsavory concoction. *Beggars can't be choosers,* Skibby thought to himself, having remembered reading it in John Heywood's 1546 collection of proverbs. And since he hadn't eaten in days, Skibby would have eaten just about anything.

"Thought you was hungry," Silas reminded him.

"For food," Skibby retorted, doing his best not to vomit the cornmeal gruel.

"Suit yourself, then," Silas replied, willingly slurping down a few more mouthfuls.

Skibby's raging hunger forced him to choke down a few more unsavory gulps before finally giving up in disgust. Satisfied and full, Silas led Skibby further through the village. As they meandered through pockets of activity, Skibby caught a glimpse of

Running Dove, who was carrying a bow and a quiver of arrows across her back. His eyes followed her, mesmerized by her distinctive appearance and movement, having never seen anyone like her.

It wasn't difficult for Silas to notice. "Don't unsettle yourself none. You leavin' anyhow, ain't you?" Silas remarked, his question snapping Skibby from his distracted gaze.

The two men stopped in a small secluded clearing a short distance from another group of men. The small contingent of Seminoles was seated on logs and stones in a loose semicircle and appeared to be in the middle of a tense conversation.

"Tribal Council," Silas explained. "Look like they talkin' serious."

Skibby wasn't paying attention. He was still enamored with Running Dove and glanced at Silas, wondering, *Did you say something?*

"Them white folks you was runnin' from," Silas reminded Skibby, "damn near led 'em straight to us."

Skibby was surprised to hear this. It seemed word of his incident with the posse had spread quickly. He shook his head, remembering something his mother had told him. "Freedom ain't always free," he mused softly.

"Not so long as there be white folks," Silas added.

The Seminole Tribal Council consisted of seven men. Ghost Bear and Crow Dog were there along with Joseph Tree, a Black Seminole who had risen through the ranks of former slaves to become a trusted leader and integral member of the tribe. Seated between Ghost Bear and Crow Dog was Great Elk, the Seminole chief who, along with his aura of authority and wisdom, at his advance age was still very fit. The Tribal Council was the tribe's governing body and met to discuss matters of importance that impacted the tribe's well-being and survival.

Crow Dog beckoned Silas, who then nudged Skibby forward. The two approached the Tribal Council and took up seats facing Great Elk at the mouth of the loose semicircle, Ghost Bear's familiar face helping to ease some of Skibby's apprehension. It was Skibby's first time seeing Ghost Bear since being rescued and prompted a respectful nod of thanks. He then turned inquisitively to Silas, who understood Skibby's unspoken question.

"Ghost Bear," Silas informed him.

Now that Skibby and Silas were seated at the council circle, Crow Dog welcomed the newcomer. "Welcome, brother. I am Crow Dog." He turned to Great Elk. "This is Great Elk, our father and chief."

Skibby was surprised to hear Crow Dog speak English and looked again to Silas.

"Yes, we speak the white man's language," Crow Dog responded, deciphering Skibby's inquisitive look.

"Better'n most white folks too," Silas added.

Great Elk spoke softly in his native Mikisúkî dialect to Skibby then repeated his question in English. "What is your name?"

"Frank Narcisse Clay. Folks call me Skibby."

"Very well, Skibby. It seems we have much in common. You seek freedom from

162

your white fathers. My people also seek to live in freedom and peace."

"This not exactly the freedom I pictured," Skibby replied, insulting the Tribal Council in the process. Their indignant stares of contempt confirmed to Skibby he had spoken out of turn.

"Perhaps Ghost Bear would have better served you by remaining hidden," Joseph Tree proffered, offended by Skibby's ill manners.

"And better served his people," interjected Crow Dog. "Ghost Bear's foolish act will only cause the white man's anger to burn more brightly."

As the discussion escalated, Ghost Bear displayed the same quiet confidence he showed the afternoon he rescued Skibby. He addressed the group, reverting to his native dialect to emphasize his point. "When we meet in battle, the white man's hatred will cloud his judgement. And our number has grown, if only by one."

The Tribal Council continued the tense discussion in their Mikisúkî dialect.

"One, at the risk of many," Crow Dog warned.

Joseph Tree panned around slowly, taking stock of the surrounding wilderness. "Perhaps it is time we move deeper into the forest."

"Or consider the treaty set forth and go west of the Big River," suggested Crow Dog.

Hearing this, Ghost Bear sprung up defiantly, Crow Dog's words grating in his ears. "I would sooner fight here and die than share lands with our enemies."

"There has been enough bloodshed," Crow Dog responded, always favoring a nonviolent solution over conflict and war. "It is time we made peace so our people may live."

"Peace does not walk on a trail of broken treaties," countered Ghost Bear, adding still more fuel to the argument.

Great Elk had been listening patiently as the men argued, quietly formulating his resolution. He raised his hand and the group fell silent to his authority. "At Payne's Landing, many of our red brothers signed the white man's treaty. Their spirit was broken. They would leave their homeland in exchange for new lands to the West. The white man's father, Sharp Knife, spoke with a forked tongue." The men nodded agreement and continued listening intently as Great Elk continued. "This treaty required that we return our dark brothers to their white masters. I would not sign the false words of the yellow hair. Now, we will stay and fight for what is rightfully ours … this land handed down by our ancestors—and our freedom." Great Elk gestured with his arm, signaling the meeting was over. The Tribal Council accepted his word as final and dispersed.

Skibby had never witnessed anything like this. He was moved by Great Elk's calm, passionate authority—by words he could not understand. Silas noticed Skibby's state of admiration and made a final appeal. "You could set off, or you could—"

Suddenly Ghost Bear appeared out of thin air, startling Skibby. Silas stopped mid-sentence, unmoved, having become accustomed to Ghost Bear's sudden ghostlike appearances.

"When the danger from your white

masters has passed, you may go. Until that time …" Ghost Bear advised Skibby.

"This here Ghost Bear," Silas announced casually.

Skibby took the opportunity to thank Ghost Bear again, this time face to face. "I reckon I owe you—"

"Nothing," Ghost Bear interrupted. "Should the time come, I hope you would do the same."

Skibby nodded, now more intrigued than ever.

II

Mamé gently tended the ghastly wounds on Topher's back as he lay face down on a pallet. "This medicine gon' ease you," she said, her voice a comfort to her ailing son. Topher winced in pain as she applied melted tallow to his newly shredded back. "It hurt now, but time gon' heal," she continued.

"Not 'til they get what comin'," Topher vowed.

"God don't like ugly, son. Get yo'self

killed thinking like that. Then who I got left?"

"We all gon' die sometime. Sooner fo' me the better."

Topher's words were alarming to Mamé, and she did her best to lead him away from his vengeful, suicidal thoughts. "We all hurtin' … but Mercy and Skibby gone. They in a better place now." She took note of the necklace around Topher's neck. "That necklace represent everything we done fought against and struggled for. You needs to think clear, maybe one day make a better life."

Topher stared blankly at the wall as Mamé's words sank in.

Standing somberly over a fresh, unmarked grave, Topher clutched a bunch of newly plucked wildflowers. He knelt slowly, wincing from his fresh wounds as he gently placed the flowers on Mercy's grave. "I promise some good gon' come from all this trouble," Topher assured his dead wife.

12

A horned owl sat perched high in a tree, basking in the sun as it spied Skibby standing below in a small clearing, a bow and arrow in his hand. Eager to shoot the owl from its perch, Skibby clumsily arched the bow to its maximum tension, trying hard to steady it before releasing the bowstring. The arrow tumbled harmlessly from the bow with a deflating *TWANG,* prompting the owl to blink apathetically.

"I had me a gun …" Skibby mused aloud, suddenly distracted by the snickering behind him. He turned to see Running Dove, who was thoroughly amused by his pathetic display of archery. "What you laughin' at?" he questioned indignantly, a poor attempt to conceal his embarrassment.

Running Dove tried in vain to suppress her giggling, and Skibby tried to appear unmoved by her presence. The look on his face betrayed him—the awkwardness of being in the presence of his heroine and hopelessly unprepared for the moment.

Ghost Bear appeared suddenly behind Skibby, as always seemingly out of thin air. He carried a bow of his own, a quiver of arrows slung over one shoulder, a leather pouch over the other. Skibby was completely oblivious to Ghost Bear's presence.

"Guns are useful at times ..." explained Ghost Bear, his voice startling Skibby and causing Running Dove to giggle even harder, adding to Skibby's embarrassment and chagrin. Wanting to be alone with Skibby, Ghost Bear motioned Running Dove away with his eyes. She acquiesced, snickering as she went.

"... but one shot, and every animal in the forest would scatter for miles," Ghost Bear explained further.

"But if—"

"And most important, guns alert enemies to our presence," Ghost Bear continued, finishing his point.

"Had enough guns, wouldn't be no enemies," Skibby scoffed, prompting Ghost Bear to eye Skibby coolly as he contemplated his words.

Ghost Bear then turned his attention to the surrounding wilderness, casually scanning the trees as he spoke. "You have adopted the white man's way of thinking."

"I hate them whites … same as you."

"Hatred clouds your vision … obscures the trail," Ghost Bear replied, pulling an arrow nonchalantly from his quiver.

"Ain't hate reason enough to kill your enemies?"

Ghost Bear smoothly loaded the arrow into his bow with great skill and precision, the result of years of training and experience. From the corner of his eye, he tracked something in the trees. "The yellow hair kills out of hatred and greed," Ghost

Bear explained, pulling back on his bow in one strong fluid motion. "The Seminole kills to protect his land," he continued, shooting skyward, the arrow hissing through the forest canopy. "And to survive."

Seconds later a large bird crashed to the ground, rendering Skibby awestruck and speechless. Ghost Bear casually pulled his arrow from the limp bird's body then wiped the bloody arrowhead on the forest undergrowth. It was all just a matter of course for him. He stashed the kill in the pouch hanging from his shoulder and slipped the arrow back into its quiver. Skibby looked admiringly at Ghost Bear's bow then indignantly at his own mediocre version.

"A useful weapon, mastered by few," Ghost Bear informed Skibby matter-of-factly. He then looked deep into Skibby's eyes, measuring, searching for some unseen quality. "If your heart is pure, you will learn the path of the warrior."

Ghost Bear set his gear down and beckoned Skibby to follow. Skibby set down his own bow and arrow, beset with apprehension yet curious what was in store.

Ghost Bear was already moving deeper into the wilderness, deftly maneuvering through the thick forest like a ghost, unmindful of Skibby scrambling to keep up. Skibby quickly fell behind as he lumbered along, struggling to follow the path Ghost Bear navigated so easily. The bugs buzzing around his face didn't make the task any easier. Skibby was completely inept in this swampy jungle and completely oblivious to the dangerous creatures lurking everywhere. He walked unwittingly through a large glistening spider web then manically tried to clear the sticky silk from his face.

Ghost Bear glanced back to check Skibby's progress, only to witness his protégé's pathetic struggle. He shook his head—somewhat amused, mostly in disgust at Skibby's ineptitude—and waited.

As Skibby made his best effort to close the distance between him and Ghost Bear, his lack of any real experience in this terrain made him unaware of the water moccasin camouflaged on the trail a few feet in front of him. As Skibby's worn boot came down unwittingly, the snake slithered away, avoiding being trampled and negating the necessity to bite Skibby on the ankle.

Skibby's heart pounded as he recoiled in fear, his head shaking at the impossible situation he found himself in. In a desperate effort to regain his composure and calm his shattered nerves, Skibby bent over, took a deep breath, then slowly exhaled his exasperation. After a brief moment, he resumed his clumsy progress along the trail, the short journey to Ghost Bear proving quite arduous. Upon reaching Ghost Bear, Skibby noticed a bunch of succulent apples hanging from a low flying branch of a manchineel tree. He immediately plucked one, intent on devouring it.

"I would not eat that," Ghost Bear warned. Skibby gazed at the fruit, his hunger mounting, then tossed it aside dejectedly. "Poison. And to think …" Realizing Skibby was incapable of following and keeping up, Ghost pointed the way, indicating that Skibby was to lead. The protégé trudged off slowly, unsure of himself, mumbling his frustration as he awkwardly navigated his way through the forest

Still muttering and wondering Ghost Bear's intentions, Skibby peeked over his shoulder. What he saw caused a gasp of shock and bewilderment. Ghost Bear, his only hope of survival, was no longer behind him. *What the hell else could possibly go wrong,* Skibby thought to himself. He scanned the wilderness nervously then noticed the sun hanging low in the sky. With daylight waning, he did what he assumed the most sensible thing: he turned back in the direction he had come.

As he carefully made his way back to what he hoped was the Seminole village, Skibby suddenly realized all the activity and ever present heat had made him thirsty. He noticed a shallow marsh and stepped down a small embankment to a shallow pool of water. Too murky to drink, he squatted down and cooled himself with a splash to his face and neck, losing himself in thought, forgetting for a moment he was hopelessly lost. Then he noticed it …

As his gaze shifted from the flat, still water to the log floating in his direction, the gears began turning in his mind. His brow furrowed, realizing he had been mistaken. The log floating toward him was in fact an alligator slyly gliding his way. Having grown up on a bayou plantation in Louisiana, Skibby was somewhat familiar alligators. As his brain made the connection, he exploded backwards out of his crouch, wild with fear. He tried desperately to scramble back up the slippery embankment, his manic attempts proving futile. The more he scrambled, the more Skibby slid back toward the approaching alligator.

Finally, the alligator reached the edge of the shallow pool and slowly lumbered out of the murky water. Skibby's fearful attempts were now an all-out panicked scramble. His heart raced as the reptile crept closer, opening its huge mouth to reveal rows of razor sharp teeth, inches from its next meal. Skibby was moments away from certain death. Silas had been right after all; the only thing for Skibby out in that wilderness was hard times and death, and he had already gotten his fill of hard times.

As the alligator prepared to snap its crushing jaws down on Skibby, Ghost Bear burst through the thick foliage, leaping effortlessly onto a sturdy vine, swinging past the alligator and snatching Skibby to safety with not a second to spare. Deprived of its next meal, the alligator turned slowly and slithered back into the soupy marsh as Skibby and Ghost Bear lay sprawled on the ground, adrenaline pumping through their veins, Skibby thankful to be alive. Not a word was spoken for several minutes as they lay there breathing heavily, their minds awhirl. And then …

"This is the second time I have saved you from danger," Ghost Bear reminded Skibby, still charged with excitement.

"Let's hope it be the last," Skibby panted.

Ghost Bear gazed at Skibby, amused and equally amazed. "You cheat death like a fox. Today I give your Seminole name …

Cvla-lvstē … Black Fox."

Skibby liked the sound of it. He let the name sink in then nodded his acceptance. Ghost Bear picked himself up and started back toward the Seminole village. Skibby scrambled to his feet and followed behind closely.

Skibby meandered through the chikees, this time with a newfound curiosity and appreciation for the Seminoles and their way of life. *I know nothing of these people, yet I sense we have much in common,* he thought to himself. As he walked through the village, he came upon scene after scene that drew his admiration: a warrior feathering an arrow, women weaving baskets from swamp cane, Ghost Bear honing his tomahawk. *I have never known such pride.* And finally, he saw Running Dove. *Or felt such feelings.*

13

FLORIDA WILDERNESS · AUGUST · 1857

A quiet stillness permeated the forest as steam rose from the moist ground on another sweltering afternoon. A dragonfly hovered about, occasionally darting from one spot to the next. Rays of sunlight filtered through the forest canopy as the same apathetic owl sat perched in a tree, watching something below. A bird frolicking in a nearby tree prompted the owl to shift its gaze.

Suddenly a *wooshing* sound preceded the explosion of feathers as an arrow skewered the unsuspecting bird and sent it crashing dead to the ground below. Unfazed, the owl swiveled its head and blinked indifferently.

In the clearing below, Skibby stood in full Seminole regalia: buckskin leggings and breechcloth, moccasins, and a man's straight shirt with a shoulder belt of woven beadwork—a Black Seminole. With his bow in hand, he glanced over his shoulder and smiled. Running Dove smiled back playfully.

Four years had passed since Mercy's death. Much happened on that day and much had happened in the years since. Skibby, no longer a hapless runaway struggling with life amongst the Seminoles, was one of them now. He had gained their trust and respect, along with his place in the tribe. He had learned the ways of the Seminole … and the path of the warrior.

The mood at Bayou Saint Claire was different too. Change was just over the horizon, and Master Jack sensed the beginning of the end of his family's way of life.

As he stood in front of the large parlor window, Master Jack admired the dramatic view of Bayou Saint Claire and all its splendor as he took the usual slow, deliberate draw on his pipe. Austin sat nearby as Rev swept in the background, pretending not to listen.

"Times are changing," Master Jack

mused. "The freedoms enjoyed by blacks in the North threaten our way of life here."

Austin shook his head in disbelief, not willing to accept his father's words. "Do we not hold dominion over niggers here in the South?" he asked excitedly.

Master Jack turned from the window, sympathetic to Austin's outburst. "I believed that once. Now, with more and more slaves inclined to be independent and free …"

"Not without a fight," Austin declared, believing his rule over slaves a God-given birthright.

"Fighting may be inevitable, son … We must be mindful. Upheaval is just around the corner," Master Jack warned, his gaze returning to what lay beyond the parlor window.

As Master Jack looked out over his plantation, Rev swept the last corner then quietly slipped away.

Topher sat in the dimly lit shanty—a silhouette against the last of the day's sunlight filtering through the window—fixated on the ancestral necklace in his hand. Rev appeared at the open door, surprised to see Topher sitting alone in the semi-dark room. He knocked then entered without waiting for an invitation.

"Trying to make yourself blind?" Rev asked.

He retrieved an oil lamp from its perch on a nearby shelf then struck a match on the rough-hewn table. Rev placed the match against the lantern's cotton wick, lighting the lamp and washing the room in a soft glowing light. He took a seat at the table across from Topher, who still hadn't acknowledged his presence. Finally, Topher finished staring at the necklace and placed it around his neck. As he did, a commotion began to stir outside. Topher and Rev exchanged curious glances then moved to the doorway to investigate.

What they saw—pandemonium and chaos, slaves running about in disarray, full of excitement—left them stunned. Topher and Rev were equally surprised to see unfamiliar faces circulating through the slave quarters. Armed with torches and a crude assortment of weapons, these unknown slaves excitedly whipped up support, urging the resident slaves to join their uprising. A few of the plantation slaves joined; most retreated to their shanties and shut themselves inside. The mob of rebellious slaves was enough to pose a significant threat to Bayou Saint Claire.

"I'll be damned," Rev uttered as he and Topher stood mesmerized in the doorway.

As the mob clamored its way toward the Big House, standing in their way was Smith, his gun drawn and cocked, a wad of tobacco in his cheek. "Ya'll niggers stop right there," he ordered, more than a little vexed. The mob heeded the order and stopped short, a fitting reaction to Smith's revolver pointing them in the face.

As the slaves stood uneasy, an unfamiliar man cautiously stepped forward, mindful he was staring down the barrel of Smith's Colt. "Stand aside, Cracker Jack," he muttered, his false bravado unconvincing. As he looked around to the other runaways for assurances, their steely looks of support confirmed that on this day they were not to be ignored.

Smith took stock of the ragtag group—every ounce of disdain in his body oozing from his grungy pores—before spitting a greasy wad of tobacco at the unfamiliar man's feet. As the rebellious slave glanced down at his tobacco-splattered shoe, the boom of Smith's gun discharging reverberated through the slave quarters, the bullet exploding into the middle of the slave's forehead, dropping him like a bag of rocks. The mob stood in stunned silence, glancing briefly at one another before charging Smith in a chaotic rage. He cocked the trigger and squeezed off another round before being overrun and plowed to the ground in a blur of pummeling clubs and fists. Smith's execution was brutal and swift, and plantation slaves peeking from doorways quickly disappeared behind closed doors, understanding that Smith's death was not something to be witness to. The mob left Smith in a bloody heap as they continued toward the Big House.

The plantation slaves weren't alone in their awareness of the emerging revolt. LaSalle, too, was privy. Hunkered down next to a shed, he brazenly fired shots at anyone unwitting enough to cross his path. As a sturdy plantation slave unknowingly ran past, LaSalle pulled the trigger, the click of his gun's misfire catching the slave's attention. Turning toward the sound, the slave saw LaSalle pointing a gun in his direction, a contemptuous smirk on his face as he cocked the trigger and squeezed again. *CLICK*—and again the gun misfired.

The brawny slave wasted no time with his opportunity, charging LaSalle like a wounded boar, buckling the hated overseer against the shed like a rag doll and sending his revolver flying. Making up for years of ill-treatment, the slave slammed LaSalle to the ground a few times for good measure then crept into the night.

Topher and Rev moved from the doorway onto the porch for a better vantage point. The mob was progressing toward to the Big House when a candle of thought lit in Topher's mind. "Stay here. Don't open up for no one," Topher ordered.

"Don't worry 'bout that. I'm too old fo' this mess," Rev assured him.

As Topher sprung off the porch and sprinted toward the Big House, Rev complied with his orders. Backing inside the doorway, he took one last peek around then latched himself inside.

From somewhere in the darkness, Topher heard a soft moan as he sped past Smith's dead body, causing him to change course and move to investigate. What he found was LaSalle floundering in the dirt, blood oozing from his nose and mouth. Topher didn't miss LaSalle's revolver lying on the ground a few feet away either.

"Help me up, boy," LaSalle demanded, struggling to his feet.

But Topher made no effort to help, too distracted by LaSalle's black Colt Walker. As LaSalle pulled himself up against the shed, he did his best to read Topher's intentions.

"Go on, boy."

Blatantly disregarding LaSalle's demand, Topher picked up the gun, which was heavier than expected, and aimed it clumsily in LaSalle's direction. Incensed, LaSalle could hardly contain his outrage at Topher's insubordination. "Damn triflin' ni—" *BOOM.* This time the gun fired. Topher's hand jolted back from the recoil as the lead bullet hit LaSalle, slamming him up against the shed. A fresh bullet hole in his chest, LaSalle slumped over as the life slowly drained from his body.

"Over your dead body," Topher whispered as he tossed the gun at LaSalle's feet. There was no joy in Topher's expression, just cold satisfaction. And he suddenly realized that with both Smith and LaSalle dead, now was his second chance at freedom. He scanned the plantation then sprinted into the darkness.

Master Jack and Austin were on high alert as they stood guard on the back porch, an assortment of rifles and guns at their disposal. Two slave men, Brodie and Sam, were there helping to load weapons and keep watch. Mamé stood anxiously inside the back door, and Celeste was just behind her out of harm's way.

As the slave mob moved closer, repetitive booms resounded. Master Jack and Austin had opened fire, not waiting to ask the mob's intentions. The advancing slaves scurried for cover, diving behind trees and bushes as smoke began wafting up from the gunfire. *BOOM*—a slave was felled advancing toward the house. Suddenly a torch flying end over end crashed onto the porch, charring the wood siding as the flames danced against the wall in the darkness. The slaves maneuvered slowly toward the Big House, using trees for cover. Master Jack, Austin, Brodie, and Sam worked diligently to keep them at bay. In the vestibule, Celeste craned forward, eager for a better view of the action.

"Miss Celeste, go on up to your room and latch the door. Now, child!" Mamé ordered excitedly. Then she rushed out the door, pulling off her apron as she went.

Celeste hadn't moved an inch toward her room. Instead, she opened the drawer of a small side table where a large revolver rested inside. She pulled the gun from the drawer and stepped out onto the porch, unnoticed through the haze and chaos. Mamé was busy smothering the torch flames lapping at the back wall with her apron. Everyone else was tensely focused on the advancing mob.

Clutching the revolver with both hands, Celeste found her way to the corner of the porch, aimed clumsily, then fired at an unfamiliar slave moving in the distance. The recoil overpowered Celeste and jolted her backwards, sending her tumbling off the side of the porch and crashing to the ground, her head hitting with a thud. As she woozily struggled to her feet, the hazy figure of an unknown black man appeared behind her. He grabbed Celeste around the neck, muffling her cries as he dragged her away.

As dawn settled on Bayou Saint Claire, a few dogs tramped back and forth between the dead slaves, sniffing bodies for any signs of life. Master Jack slept uneasily in his rocking chair, a rifle resting between his legs while Brodie and Sam sat with their backs against the wall next to him, bleary eyed from keeping watch all night.

Rays of light from the rising sun reached Master Jack's face and roused him from his tortured slumber. He looked tired and worn and seeing him awaken, Brodie and Sam stood up dutifully. It took a moment before he remembered the previous night. And then … "Sam, go and fetch Smith and

LaSalle."

"Yessa," Sam replied, nodding.

"Don't bother," Austin advised as he approached the porch, a grim look on his face.

Master Jack lifted himself out of his rocker and set his rifle aside as he looked out over the plantation … and the dead bodies. A difficult sight to bear. And a harsh reality that times were changing and that Bayou Saint Claire could well face similar upheavals in the future. A few plantation slaves milled about, sifting through the dead bodies. Discouraged, Master Jack sank back into his rocker.

"Miss Celeste not in her room. She gone!" Mamé exclaimed hysterically as she burst out the back door.

Master Jack sprung up once again

from his rocking chair, a mix of anger and concern, the situation having just gotten much worse and much closer to home. "In the name of Jesus, did anyone see her?" he questioned excitedly. Brodie and Sam shook their heads.

Mamé did her best to remember. "She was right behind me. Then I come out here to—"

"Brodie, fetch my horse. Be quick about it," Austin demanded, the tone of his voice masking his uncertainty about what exactly he would do to find Celeste.

"Yessa," Brodie answered, hurrying off toward the stable.

Master Jack's mood sank further. "We'll find you, so help me if it's the last thing," he promised wishfully—almost to himself.

"Lord have mercy," Mamé muttered in despair.

With all the commotion surrounding Celeste, the sound of heavy footsteps approaching from around the corner of the house went unnoticed. Finally, all eyes moved toward the sound that was slowly moving closer, Austin's hand instinctively jerking to his revolver. He snatched it from its holster as Master Jack grabbed his rifle, both pointing in the direction of the oncoming sound. As the footsteps moved closer, Master Jack's rifle moved to eye level.

Everyone braced themselves and waited, their tense apprehension turning to relief as Topher appeared carrying Celeste in his arms. She was dirty and disheveled, half-conscious, but alive. And it was clear by Topher's bleary eyes he'd been up all night. Both he and Celeste looked as if they'd just returned from a quick trip to Hell.

Looking up to see several sets of eyes staring at him, and especially with Master Jack and Austin's fingers on their triggers, Topher stopped dead in his tracks. He cautiously lowered Celeste to the ground, not taking his eyes off the onlookers, then dropped her in a heap and ran like hell. Master Jack focused his eye, sighting Topher down the long end of his rifle barrel, his finger on the trigger, squeezing slightly until …

BOOM. A gunshot rang out, snapping Master Jack from his intense focus. He eased his finger off the trigger, lowering his rifle as everyone's attention shifted to Austin, who's gun was smoking from the bullet he had just shot skyward. Austin watched as Topher sprinted into the distance, almost admiringly so.

"Thank you, Jesus," Mamé gasped in relief.

"Well, get after him," Master Jack bellowed at Sam, who duteously obeyed, sprinting off the porch after Topher.

Austin holstered his revolver and hustled down the porch toward Celeste, Mamé right behind him, anxious and concerned as Austin gently cradled Celeste in his arms, picked her up, and carried her up the porch steps and into the house. Master Jack collapsed back into his rocker and stared somberly into the distance, wondering how things had gotten so out of hand so quickly.

Inside the house, Austin carried

Celeste up the stairs and into her bedroom then gently placed her on top of her neatly made bed. Moments later, Mamé entered the room and placed a warm damp towel on Celeste's forehead. As Mamé removed Celeste's shoes, Austin watched lovingly for a moment then stepped back and quietly slipped away.

For the second time, Topher found himself running for his life. He sprinted blindly, crashing through the forest like a wild boar. Then, from the corner of his eye, he glimpsed something—an old run-down shack abandoned for some time and almost completely hidden in the forest growth, half of its roof missing. Topher made a beeline toward it.

Austin stood over the desk, intently viewing an official looking document. He drew a pen from its inkwell and signed the document with great intention. He then melted a dollop of red wax onto the document and imprinted the soft wax with the Clay family seal. After examining it one last time, he carefully folded the paper and stuffed it into his pocket.

Brody waited by with his horse as Austin strode resolutely onto the porch, Master Jack still slouched in his rocker, doing his best to make sense of everything. Austin stepped down the porch and took the reins from Brodie just as Sam was returning from his mission to locate Topher.

"Well?" questioned Master Jack.

"He not far. Headin' out past Adams Creek ... ol' shack out that way," Sam answered, out of breath from having just run a few miles out and back.

"You want I go wit you, Massa?" asked Brodie.

"Yes, why don't you. Last thing we need is another mishap," suggested Master Jack, not wanting lose anything more that day, be it family or property.

But this was something Austin needed to do alone. "I can handle it," he said flatly.

Master Jack conceded and leaned back into his rocker, a host of emotions swirling in his head. Austin jumped aboard his horse and determinedly galloped off after Topher.

Sitting against a wall, exhausted, Topher tried in vain to stay awake and alert. His eyelids betrayed him, growing heavy... and slowly closing.

Following the path Topher cleared on his escape, Austin soon came upon the abandoned shack. He stopped some distance away and did his best to dismount quietly then slowly drew his gun.

Topher's eyelids flashed open at the sound of footsteps approaching. He sprang up, panicked, and frantically searched for something, anything to use as a weapon. His heart racing, Topher settled on a grungy plank of wood, doing his best not to make a sound picking it up. He was sweating heavily now—the sweat of fear.

The footsteps grew closer and closer … and then stopped. Topher raised the plank with both hands now, ready to strike, listening, waiting motionless. The suspense proved too much however, and he cautiously poked his head out the opening where a door used to hang. *CLICK*. Austin's gun cocked … and was pointed directly at Topher's temple. The plank of wood dropped from Topher's grip and clanged to the ground, his arms raised in surrender.

"And here we are, yet again," Austin reflected aloud. "I'd be within my rights to…"

Topher hadn't moved. His stillness and expression conveyed his mental resignation and his physical surrender. Finally, his arms lowered. "Get on wit it, then."

"Considering all you've put us through." Austin holstered his gun and retrieved the document from his pocket. "We took something from you … and you gave us something back." He stuffed the paper into Topher's hand and looked the slave in the eye. "We'll call it even," Austin declared as he turned and walked away, satisfied that against his beliefs, he had done the right thing. He climbed aboard his horse and galloped off through the forest, not bothering to look back.

Topher slowly unfolded the handwritten document and did his best to read it:

Know all men to whom these presents shall come that I, Austin Samuel Clay of the Parish

of Lafourche in the state of Louisiana, do consent to the manumission of my nigger named Christopher Narcisse Clay, about thirty years of age, to act and provide for himself as a freeman, on this twenty third day of August in the year of our Lord, One Thousand and Eight Hundred and Fifty-Seven.
—*Samuel Austin Clay.*

Many of the words were foreign, but Topher knew well enough what a freedom paper looked like. He glanced up in astonishment, but Austin was long gone.

14

The army encampment was set deep in the
Florida wilderness in a large clearing. Topher
stood in loose formation with a ragtag group
of black men: fifty newly recruited militia
standing at undisciplined attention. Some
carried weapons; most were without. Major
Thomason was on horseback flanked by two
younger mounted officers, facing the Black
Regiment. Topher glanced down at the piece
of paper he was clutching then folded it
up and stuffed it into his pocket, a serious,

determined look on his face—a sense of purpose.

Cole, the pitiful looking man next to Topher was jovial in contrast. He gave Topher a nudge. "Name's Cole."

Not to be bothered, Topher gave his own name flatly.

The Black Regiment's ragged appearance was in stark contrast to Major Thomason and his fellow officers' crisp military uniforms. He was all business and addressed the group matter-of-factly. "You've been volunteered for service in the Southern Militia's Black Regiment. You belong now to the United States Army and will obey orders as such. Any insubordination will be dealt with accordingly," he said, glancing at a noose hanging in a nearby tree, reminding the black men of their status. "At the end of your service, those of you still breathing will be granted certain liberties previously unavailable to you." The black men glanced around at each other, unsure of Major Thomason's meaning. "In other words, you'll be granted your freedom," he explained.

The Black Regiment cheered as Cole nudged Topher again. "Hear that? After this we's free."

"Already is," Topher responded coolly. Cole eyed him, puzzled by this revelation.

A militiaman raised his hand with a question. "You there," Major Thomason said as he pointed the man out.

"How long 'til we's free?"

"Until the task at hand is complete," the major responded. "We've been charged with removal of the Seminole Indians to the Oklahoma Territories. Hostiles neither willing nor cooperative." The black men glanced around again, commenting on this news. "Reveille sounds tomorrow at dawn," Major Thomason continued. "I suggest you use this free time wisely. Dismissed," he barked, watching unimpressed as the shabby group disassembled.

As the day wound down, the Black Regiment shared a quiet moment, scattered amidst their tents in small groups, lounging idly, chatting, playing cards. Topher sat on an empty crate with a small mirror in one hand, a razor in the other, his face lathered with soap. Cole was there, silently observing. Topher carefully shaved his beard until his face was a smooth finish, barely recognizable. He was clean shaven for the first time in years. He massaged the smooth skin then turned and accepted Cole's nod of approval.

Several campfires flickered in the darkness as Joseph Tree rapidly made his way through the Seminole village. He arrived at a campfire where Skibby was in conversation with the Tribal Council, his four years living with the Seminoles having forced him out of necessity to learn their language. The Seminoles no longer needed to speak English for Skibby, but they could no longer speak their native tongue to conceal things from him either.

Joseph Tree reported to the group. "Tribes are moving west to the Oklahoma Territories. Swift Arrow is camped with twenty men at Cypress Knee."

"We would be wise to join forces,"

suggested Crow Dog.

Great Elk responded, "Tomorrow you will seek out Swift Arrow. Together we will wage war against the white intruders."

In nearly perfect Mikisúkî dialect, Skibby spoke. "I am not from here, but this land has given me freedom. I believe there is honor in this fight."

Nodding his approval of Skibby's dialect, Great Elk continued. "There are no shades of gray in the matter of justice. There is only right and wrong. So, we will defend our freedom with truth..." he glanced at Skibby "...and honor."

Without celebration, the Tribal Council nodded approval of Great Elk's words.

Major Thomason sat quietly atop his horse, a young soldier on horseback next to him. Several other officers were at the ready, some on horseback, some on foot. The young soldier snapped a bugle to his lips and sounded reveille.

A slow hint of movement filtered through the clearing. Gradually, the entire camp was a clamor of activity. Soldiers moved about with purpose, hurriedly preparing for deployment. Tents were collapsed, fires doused, and wagons loaded. There seemed to be a method to the madness.

Satisfied the camp was sufficiently

broken down and the soldiers prepared to depart, Major Thomason nodded his go-ahead to the bugler, who snapped to and sounded the assembly call. The troops scurried to form ranks. It was quite an assemblage: foot soldiers, mounted officers, wagons, horse drawn cannons, black militiamen, and native scouts. The troops numbered 250 in all.

Major Thomason signaled again, this time the bugler sounding the call to move out. Four Creek scouts led the way on foot with Major Thomason close behind as the huge assemblage began moving out of camp. Falling in behind Major Thomason were eight mounted officers, three companies of the U.S. Army's Fourth Infantry, the Black Regiment, supply wagons, and cannons.

15

Crow Dog, Ghost Bear, and three other warriors made preparations to visit Swift Arrow, leader of a nearby band of Seminoles. They checked bows and tomahawks and filled quivers with arrows. Sufficiently armed, the warriors departed the village as Great Elk nodded his blessing.

The five warriors moved in single file swiftly along a narrow trail. They eventually arrived at Swift Arrow's camp, completely unfazed at having just run several miles to get there. As they filtered into the camp, the first thing they noticed were the few smoldering campfires and makeshift shelters—a sign the camp had been hastily abandoned. Fanning out, the warriors moved toward the center of the clearing, inspecting cautiously. Their instincts, honed to a knife's edge over generations, were sending signals that something was amiss. The Seminole's mood was uneasy.

As the Seminoles carefully investigated the camp, an arrow whizzed in and pierced one of them in the back, exploding out through his heart. The warrior stood frozen, eyes wide before he crumpled to the ground, dead.

The four remaining Seminoles spun around defensively, scanning the tree line, quickly nocking bows. Before they could do so, a second arrow screamed in and pierced a warrior through the neck. Two Seminoles lay dead in the blink of an eye.

Suddenly, seven Creek warriors poured into the clearing on a wave of whoops and war cries, tomahawks and war clubs in hand, feathers flying. The Seminoles unloaded their bows at the onslaught, sending two Creeks plowing headlong into the ground, dead. The remaining five Creeks crashed into the Seminoles in a flash of tomahawks and war clubs, initiating a fierce hand-to-hand battle.

The Seminoles did their best to form a tight defensive circle. They fought valiantly to stave off the Creeks, but their efforts were becoming hopeless.

Suddenly, Joseph Tree, Skibby, and

three additional Seminole warriors swarmed in on a crescendo of war cries, a blur of war clubs and hatchets and knives scalping. The ensuing battle was vicious and bloody, but the Seminoles managed to turn the tables, brutally finishing off the five Creek warriors. Standing victoriously amongst the dead bodies, the bloodied and battered Seminoles were breathing hard—and not without their own casualties. Four Seminoles lay dead, including Crow Dog.

Skibby stood silently with Ghost Bear at the edge of the Seminole village, Ghost Bear turning to Skibby to speak. "Black Fox, today you experienced battle for the first time. This time, it is I who owe you my life." Skibby acknowledged with a respectful nod. "Although born of different fathers, today we become brothers," Ghost Bear continued, extending his hand to Skibby. The two men clasped wrists, affirming their new brotherhood, then Ghost Bear turned and headed back into the village, leaving Skibby alone with his thoughts.

Skibby stood in a beautiful light, silhouetted against the setting sun, gazing out over the everglade. *I wonder where the years have gone ... and why I've come to be here. I realize now that freedom is a spiritual place, and the answer to my question is simple. I've come here to live amongst my brothers,* he thought to himself.

Joseph Tree led a horse pulling a travois

piled with fur pelts as he, Skibby, and Ghost Bear navigated their way through the marshy wilderness, soon arriving at a large hollow tree trunk—a marker in the forest. Ghost Bear retrieved a large silver medallion from the pouch slung over his shoulder and angled it against the sunlight, creating a series of bright flashes, then waited … Before long, the three men witnessed a similar series of flashes in the distance and moved out in that direction.

After a short time finding their way through the forest, the Seminoles came upon three Spanish men. Traders. The Spanish traders greeted the Seminoles respectfully but cordially. This was not their first encounter, and after the brief reintroductions, the Seminoles sat and watched patiently as the traders produced rifles and ammunition from wooden crates. The traders presented the rifles to the Seminoles, who in turn inspected the weapons, cocking triggers and checking gun sights. Satisfied, the Seminoles presented the fur pelts, which the Spaniards examined thoroughly, feeling for softness and warmth. Nods of approval signified a successful trade. Now that business had concluded, one of the traders lit a large cigar and took a long, relishing puff. He passed the cigar around, the Spaniards and Seminoles savoring both its flavor and the moment.

Skibby, Ghost Bear, and Joseph Tree navigated the trail back to their village, the travois loaded with the rifles and ammo they had traded for. Without warning, Ghost Bear motioned to stop then signaled to Joseph Tree, who quickly scaled a tree to scout the area.

Perched high in the tree, Joseph Tree could see the vast Florida wilderness for miles. He also had a close-up view of the army column only yards away, marching south toward the Seminole village. Although well equipped, the army was inept in this environment, their heavy carts and cannons lumbering through the rugged terrain.

Alarmed at what he'd just seen, Joseph Tree quickly descended the tree to report his findings. "Soldiers ... moving slow, toward the village!" he whispered.

Ghost Bear frowned in anger. "Numbers?"

"Two hundred."

Ghost Bear contemplated the intel then beckoned Skibby and Joseph Tree.

Leaving the horse and travois, they adroitly crept on their haunches through a dense thicket, slowly parting the shrubbery for a closer look at the army column clamoring past. The soldiers were so close the Seminoles could see the whiskers on their faces and smell their unfamiliar scent. They watched in silence, resentful of the intruders.

Finally, Skibby had seen enough and deemed it necessary to act, pulling an arrow from his quiver and quickly nocking it into his bow. As he focused his attention back to the passing soldiers, the Black Regiment began passing in front of him. Skibby slumped in disappointment. He was shocked to see black men marching alongside white soldiers and watched in amazement, not recognizing his own brother as Topher passed in front of him. Skibby turned aghast to Joseph Tree, who was scowling back at him, angry that Skibby would carelessly endanger them by firing his bow. Having seen enough himself, Ghost Bear signaled their retreat. The Seminoles slowly backed out of the thicket, careful not to broadcast their presence, and moved to a safe distance back at the horse and travois.

"If you must die today, it will be alone," Joseph Tree warned, whispering so as not to be heard by the passing soldiers. Skibby barely acknowledged Joseph Tree, still shaken at the sight of black men marching with the army.

"The time for fighting will arrive soon enough," Ghost Bear assured them.

"And for killing our black brothers?" Skibby questioned.

"Who would just as soon kill us for

their own freedom," countered Joseph Tree.

Which was precisely the U.S. Government's intention: dividing and conquering by pitting slave against Seminole in their struggle for freedom and justice.

"Freedom not always free," Skibby muttered to himself.

The Seminoles waited until the army column had passed and was well out of earshot. Then Joseph Tree grabbed the reins and signaled the horse forward. The three moved out with purpose, somber to the implications of the army so close to their village ... and Skibby somber to the implications of fighting against fellow black men.

The entire Seminole village had gathered around a roaring campfire, their faces lit against the dancing fire light. War drums pounded out a steady beat as some of the villagers performed a sacred war dance. In the midst of the ritual, Great Elk stood and raised his hands, drawing everyone's attention. The dancers stopped as the drums softened to a low pulse.

Great Elk sat back down to address the villagers. "Once upon a time, our ancestors roamed free over this land. They hunted and fished and harvested crops with sovereignty. Now, our future is clouded by an enemy that comes like the summer rains. Today they trespass our lands and move toward our village." The villagers were visibly unsettled and a small commotion erupted. Great Elk raised his arms, signaling for calm. "Many of our red brothers have become like the people who would drive us off this land. They will not help us in this fight. Tomorrow we will strike our village and move safe from the reach of these intruders … and we will spill the blood of our enemies."

The campsite erupted with whoops and yelps of joy at Great Elk's words. The drums again built to a loud, steady beat and the war dance resumed. As the Seminoles rejoiced, Skibby turned and made his way away from the roaring campfire, the thought of black soldiers fresh in his mind.

With war drums beating in the background, Running Dove sat alone in a chikee, her beautiful face softly illuminated by a flickering fire as she meticulously braided her long black hair.

A few small fires flickered as the Black Regiment sat scattered in groups, the silence tainted by the faint sound of the beating war drums in the distance. Topher and Cole sat listening quietly, wondering about their unseen, unknown enemy—wondering from where they would draw the courage to fight. Topher thumbed his necklace and for him the answer was clear.

"Hear that? Injuns. Too close you ask me," Cole remarked, breaking the evening's silence. Topher nodded distractedly, his mind working to find a higher purpose to his own presence there. "How come you's free anyhow?" Cole asked.

Topher pondered the question. "I brought back somethin' that meant a lot to someone," he answered, finally letting his wondering mind rest.

"Musta been real valuable you get yo' freedom. And you come here?"

"I made a promise," Topher explained.

"I was free, this the last place I'd be," replied Cole.

But Topher was gone again, lost in thought.

16

A somber mood hung over the Seminole village. Men, women, and children packed belongings and loaded them onto several travois. Goodbyes were said as twenty-five warriors prepared for battle, filling quivers, loading rifles, applying war paint to faces and bodies. Ghost Bear, Skibby, and Joseph Tree were amongst them, Skibby wrestling in his mind the battle to come.

As Skibby made preparations,

Running Dove approached quietly. She looked into Skibby's eyes lovingly as she stuffed something into his hand, gently closing his fingers around it. Then she turned and walked away, her coolness concealing her true emotions. Skibby opened his hand to find a small section of braided black hair. His gaze returned to Running Dove, and he watched affectionately as she walked away.

Several male tribe members, both native and black, escorted the women and children out of the village to a new location deeper in the wilderness. Their father and chief, Great Elk, was amongst them. The fearsome group of warriors set out in the opposite direction, armed and resolute, ready for war.

Ghost Bear and Joseph Tree led Skibby and the rest of the war party, made up of the tribe's best native and black warriors, toward the army column that was moving toward their abandoned village. Several, including Skibby had handprints painted on their bodies, signifying past hand-to-hand combat. The brand on Skibby's upper left arm was now covered with a thick leather band. Carrying the rifles newly acquired from the Spanish traders, the warriors moved assiduously through the swamp, swiftly and silently ... hardly disturbing a single blade of grass.

The army troops trudged along in formation, rifles shouldered, struggling against the intense heat and unforgiving terrain, lulled to distraction, oblivious to the danger headed their way. Horses labored to pull the heavy cannons and supply wagons through the marsh. Aside from the clamor of the army column, the forest was silent ... until ...

A flurry of arrows streaked through the sky, instantly felling several unfortunate soldiers. Mounted officers were sent tumbling from their horses as alarm and chaos rippled through the army's ranks. Amidst shouts of dismay, troops scrambled into defensive positions, frantically taking up arms, crouching, scanning the forest nervously for any signs of the enemy.

Several rifles boomed in unison as the Seminoles poured a tremendous barrage of rifle fire into the massed army ranks, cutting down several more soldiers. Horses reared in panic as chilling war cries echoed through the forest. The Seminoles fired indiscriminately into the army formation, killing soldiers at will. The soldiers, panicked with confusion, returned fire blindly into the dense woods, doing their best to aim at the muzzle flashes twinkling in the distance. As the army pumped several more volleys in scattered directions, the Seminoles ducked behind trees, easily avoiding the incoming salvo.

To the rear of the army column, a canon was hurriedly spun into position and readied. *BOOM* ... a puff of smoke streaked with fire exploded from the muzzle. The twelve-pounder ripped through the trees and foliage ... Then another. The remaining officers urgently tried to restore order, barking commands amidst the chaos.

"Cease fire! Cease fire!" Major Thomason shouted above the noise and confusion as the Seminole gunfire slackened then ceased altogether.

As the everglade fell silent, the soldiers nervously awaited the next Seminole volley. It never sounded. The Seminoles were quietly retreating deeper into the forest. The few remaining officers rallied a handful of soldiers and the Creek scouts and hurriedly deployed them into the surrounding wilderness. Advancing cautiously, they diligently searched for any signs of the Seminoles' retreat, but quickly gave up, confounded. The Seminoles had vanished and left no trace.

Satisfied the immediate threat was over, the army slowly regrouped and assessed the damage: many infantry and militia killed, several wounded, and four officers dead. The dead and wounded were soberly tended to as a grim reality began to set in. War with the Seminoles would be no picnic.

The soldiers forged ahead on another brutally hot day, this time scattered haphazardly, no longer marching in formation, their rifles at the ready. They eventually arrived at a narrow river and followed it downstream, searching for an adequate place to cross.

A few miles downstream, the river finally narrowed to a shallow crossing where a mounted officer rode in, his horse splashing as it tromped back and forth. The officer scanned the tree line, his noble effort to avert another ambush. Satisfied there was no imminent threat, he nodded, giving the all clear. A second officer gave the command, prompting soldiers to begin filtering across the river a few at a time, alert but unaware of the Seminoles lurking in the denseness on the opposite side.

As the first few soldiers neared the opposite bank, an arrow hissed in and pierced one of them in the heart. He fell to his knees, his eyes rolling back into his head before he slammed face-first into the shallow water. Before the army could react, the Seminoles unloaded a volley of arrow and rifle fire, littering the river with dead soldiers.

As the river flowed red, the few soldiers closest to the opposite side raced up the bank and charged recklessly with fixed bayonets through the swamp and scrub, their rifle fire scattering the Seminoles in several directions. A soldier's bullet found its mark … then another. Retreating Seminoles were sent sprawling as they sprinted away, one of whom was Joseph Tree. Struck by a soldier's bullet, he slammed into the marsh, hot lead lodged in the middle of his back. On a dead run, Skibby and Ghost Bear glanced back over their shoulders for Joseph Tree, but it was too late. Their comrade was surrounded by a group of soldiers and there was nothing anyone could do to change his inexorable fate.

As Joseph Tree tried to crawl away, Skibby and Ghost Bear watched helplessly as a soldier pressed his boot into Joseph Tree's back.

"Look like your days bein' free is over."

Joseph Tree struggled to pull himself free then did his best to speak. "Somethin' to say, boy?" the soldier questioned, relinquishing his foothold on the wounded

Seminole.

The soldier's boot gone, Joseph Tree was able to pull himself up onto his side. He glared at the soldier disdainfully then sealed his fate. "You will all die here."

The soldier's smirk turned to a frown as he plunged his bayonet into Joseph Tree's chest. Skibby and Ghost Bear winced, helpless to do anything for the fallen warrior, then turned and sprinted deeper into the wilderness.

17

Having regrouped, the remaining Seminoles were gliding single file along a game trail through a dense hammock. They quickly outdistanced the soldiers and soon spilled into a clearing. Fifty yards to the opposite side was another dense hammock fronted by a shallow marsh thick with tall sawgrass and bamboo. The Seminoles wasted no time sprinting toward the hammock and within moments reached the marsh. They sloshed through the shallow water then scattered into the densely wooded forest beyond. A lookout deftly scaled a tree for a better vantage point as the remaining warriors took up strategic positions, hunkered down, and waited. Skibby gazed up to see an owl perched overhead. It blinked back apathetically, bringing the slightest of smiles to Skibby's face.

After some time, the army slowly emerged from the woods on the opposite side of the clearing. Two hundred soldiers formed a line of battle along the tree line. Even though struggling with fatigue, the army was daunting in its sheer numbers. They outnumbered the Seminoles ten to one.

Once the army's entire Fourth Infantry had filtered into the clearing and settled, Major

Thomason beckoned the four Creek scouts forward with a wave. The Creeks crouched as they advanced cautiously across the open field, bows loaded and drawn. High above in the hammock, the Seminole lookout spied the advancing scouts. Using hand signals, he relayed information to his fellow warriors below ... *Four scouts advancing. Creek. Two hundred soldiers assembling for battle.*

"Today, we find our destiny," Ghost Bear informed his fellow Seminoles.

The advancing Creeks arrived at the shallow marsh, scanning the trees, ever watchful. They conferred silently then cautiously retreated backwards, their eyes glued to the tree line. Back at the army battle line, the Creeks reported their findings.

Major Thomason and his officers huddled in conference as they received the intelligence. His decision made, Major Thomason signaled a junior officer who then barked a command.

The First Company of soldiers and the thirty-five remaining members of the Black Regiment commenced forward. The Second Company fell in thirty yards behind, and the Third Company remained at the tree line, held in reserve. The advancing soldiers scattered in small groups as they moved cautiously across the clearing. At the marsh, they slowly plodded in, disappearing into the tall bamboo and sawgrass. As the tall grass swayed from soldiers moving through it, the Seminoles watched, anticipating …

Soldiers and militia slowly emerged

from the marsh, pausing on the solid ground of the hammock to collect themselves and get their bearings, acutely aware of their dangerous surroundings and the ever present threat of attack.

And like clockwork, the ambush the soldiers feared began. The first arrow hissed in and pierced a soldier in the chest. A split second later, before the soldier had even hit the ground, a swarm of arrows whooshed in, followed by a barrage of rifle fire. As their war cries echoed through the forest, the Seminole assault ripped through the army's ranks, cutting down several of the Black Regiment and First Company. A few terrified former slaves splashed cowardly back through the marsh toward the advancing Second Company, their fear of death at the hands of the Seminoles clouding their memory of the punishment they would now face.

Suddenly the boom of a cannon blast resounded, followed by an iron cannonball ripping through the trees, blowing the Seminole lookout from his perch. Frustrated by yet another ambush, Major Thomason gave the order and the Third Company began advancing rapidly across the clearing.

As the Black Regiment and First Company began filtering into the hammock, the Second Company, having arrived at the edge of the marsh, dropped to their knees and took up shooting positions.

BOOM. Another cannon blast sounded. The twelve-pounder slammed into the hammock, exploding forest and earth, blowing Seminoles to bits. Outmanned and under bombardment, the Seminoles began a desperate retreat amidst the blood and chaos. Ghost Bear and a few others remained to provide cover, slowly working their way backwards from tree to tree, maneuvering to make their tactical escape. They were soon scattered far and wide, cut off from one another, and isolated.

As two soldiers combed the bush for Seminoles, a figure sprung at them from the undergrowth. Ghost Bear was a blur, his tomahawk swinging, easily killing the unwitting soldiers with two skillful blows. He slid the tomahawk into a leather band around his waist, scanned the forest coolly, then disappeared back into the undergrowth.

In another part of the hammock in a

small clearing, Skibby was engaged with an equally determined soldier in vicious hand-to-hand combat. As they wrestled for control of the soldier's rifle, it discharged suddenly, sending a targetless bullet ripping through the forest. After a long struggle, Skibby finally managed to dislodge the rifle and slice deep into the soldier's midsection with his knife—which only encouraged the soldier to fight even harder.

The two men tussled viciously, scrapping and clawing with every bit of strength they could muster. In the blur of combat, Skibby's knife fell opportunistically to the ground, both men diving frantically after it, both trying desperately to gain the upper hand. In the fierce scuffle, Skibby managed to win the knife, but in doing so lost the advantage. The soldier's arm was suddenly clamped around Skibby's neck, squeezing tightly in a deadly throat lock.

As Skibby struggled to breathe, his fingers slowly opened and the knife dropped harmlessly from his hand. His eyes rolled back into his head, the life slowly draining from his body. The agony of being suffocated would be over soon. With his life hanging by a thread, Skibby strained his head forward slowly … then thrust it back, the forceful blow crushing the soldier's nose.

The soldier reeled, releasing his death grip as sharp, agonizing pains from his nasal cavity shot through the rest of his body. Skibby seized his chance, quickly scooping up the knife and deftly maneuvering behind his foe. The soldier gasped in pain as Skibby forced the blade deep into his liver. As Skibby shifted his arm downward, the enemy soldier slid lifelessly off his blade and crashed to the ground with a thud.

Spinning suddenly to counter another attack, Skibby found he was seconds too late. A fighter from the Black Regiment eagerly drove all twelve inches of his bayonet into Skibby's belly. Skibby's eyes sprung wide at the shock of cold steel penetrating his abdomen, a flash of recognition as he looked into his attacker's eyes. As he sagged to the ground, Skibby grabbed a handful of the enemy's shirt sleeve, which tore away to reveal an arm branded with the letters *B-S-C*.

"Topher," Skibby moaned.

Topher fell to his knees in shock, disbelieving his own ears. He reluctantly pulled down the leather band around Skibby's arm, afraid of what he might find. His fears confirmed, he shuddered at the unthinkable horror. "Skibby," he uttered grimly, cradling Skibby's head, desperately willing his brother to stay alive.

As Topher held his brother, Ghost Bear suddenly burst through the dense forest, intent on killing more soldiers. As he swooped in for the attack—a blur of color, hair roach and feathers—Ghost Bear noticed it was Skibby dying in Topher's arms. He also noticed the grief in Topher's eyes and the matching brands on the brothers' arms. Ghost Bear understood their connection and quickly took up a defensive position, scanning for enemy soldiers.

"Massa … say you was dead," Topher whispered softly, trying to find a way past his devastation.

Skibby mustered a weak smile as he gazed up at Topher. "Don't unsettle yourself none, brother. I was more alive than ever," he gasped, struggling to breath.

Topher pulled the ancestral necklace from around his neck and gently placed it around Skibby's. Skibby nodded as best he could, affirming their unspoken understanding.

Just then, another Seminole warrior burst through the forest and skidded on his knees next to Skibby and Topher. The warrior looked at Skibby horrified then removed their headband, a long mane of black hair falling out. It was Running Dove.

Skibby gazed up at her lovingly. "I'm sorry … not about choosin' you," he said, fighting hard to stay alive.

Running Dove smiled back at Skibby sadly. "It was I who chose you," she said in English. Then she spoke to Skibby in her native dialect. "Now, go and find your freedom."

Skibby's eyes closed slowly as he took his last breath. Then, just as fast as they had arrived, Ghost Bear and Running Dove tore out of the small clearing and disappeared back into the forest. Topher was alone with Skibby now, alone with his devastation. He pulled Skibby close and gently rocked his brother back and forth.

The owl, having seen everything from the safety of the canopy, blinked its usual slow blink, this time with a sense of sadness and empathy.

18

The day started like any other on the plantation, except this one would prove to be different. Topher rode through the iron gates of Bayou Saint Claire, seasoned from battle, twenty pounds lighter—his demeanor changed along with his appearance. He was not the same man that left the plantation several months earlier, and he wore that pride on his sleeve.

As Topher made his way to the stable,

slaves laboring in the fields noticed and stopped their work, gawking in astonishment, many of them having assumed Topher dead. They straightened up as they watched, proud of his freedom and the hope it gave them. The same three slave boys from his earlier return in chains excitedly took up chase alongside Topher's horse.

Master Jack rocked in his chair in his usual spot, idling the day away, his face hidden behind a newspaper. Celeste sat nearby on the porch steps, entertaining herself with her rag doll. She glanced up and sprung forth with excitement, the sight of Topher riding toward the outbuildings stealing her attention. "Topher's home," she shouted with excitement.

The back door flung open suddenly, giving way to Mamé bursting onto the back porch and racing to greet Topher. Master Jack peered over his paper to see what all the commotion was about then went back to reading, indifferent to the current proceedings.

Topher stopped at the stable and slowly looked around at the plantation, recalling the familiar surroundings … and the hardships. He had barely climbed down from his horse before the three slave boys arrived to give him an excited hug. He then turned to Mamé, who was waiting slightly out of breath, and hugged her next. Their embrace was long and heartfelt—the maternal connection between mother and son. As the memory of Skibby and Mercy sifted into his thoughts, Topher rested his head on Mamé's shoulder and softly wept as the three boys led his horse into the stable.

"I'm glad you home, son," she declared, comforting her weeping son.

The flames from the fireplace flickered in the near darkness until a pair of soft worn hands lit a lantern, washing the shack in a glowing light—the same shack once shared by Topher, Skibby, and Mercy. Mamé set the lantern down on the table as Topher sat watching, racked by guilt, wondering where he would summon the courage to tell Mamé the truth about Skibby.

"It's good you back, son. Next time don't keep me waitin' so long."

"I won't, Mamma."

"Look like you could use some of yo'

mamma's cookin'.'"

Topher barely mustered a nod as
Mamé spooned a bowlful of greens from the
cast iron pot resting over the fire. Having
filled it to her satisfaction, Mamé set the
bowl on the table and gently took up the
seat opposite her malnourished son. His
hunger overpowering his sorrow and guilt,
Topher wasted no time gulping down a few
mouthfuls. As he shoveled in his first decent
meal in months, a glance around the cabin
reminded Topher of his former life.

"What about it? You through with all
this fightin'?" Mamé asked, sensing Topher's
angst. "Seem like no good come from it."

Topher nodded, somewhat ashamed,
understanding fully the consequences of war
and the price of freedom.

As Topher continued gulping down the greens, Mamé noticed the pendant missing from around his neck. And she knew there was only one other place it could possibly be. "Where your necklace done gone?" she questioned, Topher's reaction confirming her suspicions. Her intuition told her that Skibby had been alive. Now she knew for certain her youngest son was dead. "I sure hope Skibby made somethin' of hisself," she said, the sorrow evident in her voice.

Topher glanced up at Mamé with surprise, unable to find the words to respond. But there was really nothing to be said. Mamé stood up, gently resting her hand on Topher's shoulder, then smiled softly, leaving Topher to his thoughts. Outside, she sat down on the porch steps and gazed heartbroken into the darkness.

Topher stood silently over Mercy's grave, alone with his thoughts. Finally, he placed the wildflowers he'd been clutching on the shallow mound of dirt. He had failed to fulfill his promise to her, but there was still time.

"Mr. Topher," Celeste called out as she walked up beside him. He glanced at Celeste, not answering as they both looked solemnly at Mercy's grave. After a moment, Celeste said what she had come to tell Topher. "I never thanked you for bringing me home."

"Ain't nothin'," Topher shrugged.

"I'm sorry about Miss Mercy too."

"She ain't deserve this," Topher responded, his gaze moving from her grave out over the cotton fields.

"I really am sorry, Mr. Topher."

"Me too. 'Bout a lot a things."

Celeste looked up at Topher apologetically then turned and slowly walked away.

Master Jack limped along the porch with his cane and settled into his rocker, quickly burying himself in his newspaper. The last few years had worn on him, evidenced by his tired, frayed appearance.

Topher was already sitting on the porch steps, waiting. He looked over his shoulder, hoping to get Master Jack's attention. Finally, he cleared his throat. "Ahem, Massa."

Master Jack didn't bother looking up from his paper. "I'm not your master. I expect you can look after yourself now."

"I recon so … Massa?"

Master Jack could see that whatever Topher wanted, his former slave wasn't going away until he got it. As Master Jack begrudgingly set his newspaper down, Topher was already moving toward him in a slow, deliberate manner.

"What is it Topher? Freedom not all you expected?"

"Well, suh, 'bout Skibby."

"What about him?" Master Jack inquired, his ire beginning to percolate.

"You said dem Injuns killed him."

"What you gettin' at, boy?" Master Jack questioned, his temper rising more.

Although now a free man, Topher was still well aware he was stepping into dangerous territory. He forged ahead anyway. "That ain't true."

"What the hell does that have to do with me?"

"Everything," Topher responded brazenly.

Master Jack was incredulous, not taking kindly at all to where the conversation was heading. He stood with his cane to face Topher, who by now had moved directly in front of him. "I will not stand here and be insulted, on my own property no less," Master Jack declared indignantly.

Topher no longer seemed in control of his own body and his fingers began curling subconsciously. As his fist floated upward, a worn, delicate hand touched his arm and lowered it to his side. "No, son, show some respect…" Mamé said, pausing briefly, "… to your father," she continued, almost inaudible.

Master Jack's unrepentant glare confirmed Mamé's words. Topher's heart sank as a lifetime of clues to his parentage flashed before him. He turned hastily and stumbled down the porch steps, stunned at the words that had just pierced his ears.

Mamé had come to Bayou Saint Claire in 1823 at the age of fifteen, ten years Master Jack's junior. A fragile young girl, she had nothing save the ragged denim smock she was wearing and the ancestral necklace she had been given by her mother, her only living relative and the parent she was separated from when Master Jack purchased her off the auction block. Separation from her mother had left her without benefit of a guardian, a child fending for herself in an unforgiving adult world. Master Jack had seen her at the slave auction and knew immediately he must have her as a slave to command—and as his paramour. He was instantly drawn to her mulatto features and coloring, and Master Jack's own marriage was no deterrent to his attempts to sway young Mamé in his favor. He was consumed by her presence and when sway proved unsuccessful, he resorted to coercion, forcing himself on the adolescent slave girl, having his way with her as he pleased. Mamé bore her master two illegitimate sons, both of whom curried favor with him—a denial Master Jack would perpetuate for decades. Over time, Mamé's disdain for Master Jack became loathe acceptance, possibly even admiration and gratitude. She was grateful to have her sons with her on the plantation and for the tolerant treatment they all received.

As the sun made its slow journey over the horizon the following morning, Mamé stood on the back porch, wiping her hands on her apron, watching as Topher climbed the porch steps toward her. After giving his mother a long tight embrace, he stepped back down the porch and climbed aboard his horse, pulling the colt around to face Mamé as she took a step closer.

"I wish you'd think 'bout stayin'," she declared.

Topher's forced smile told her *no*. He knew he was never coming back. Mamé knew it too.

"Where ya headin' off to?" she asked.

"Where I can make things right," Topher replied.

The moment was bittersweet—a mother losing her son to the duty he felt compelled to fulfill—and Mamé did her best not to show it. Topher reined his horse away from the porch and gave it a nudge to the ribs. The colt responded with an easy trot, and Topher rode through the iron gates, out of Bayou Saint Claire for the last time. Mamé watched for a moment then turned and headed back into the house.

19

Topher sat atop his horse, softly gripping the reins with one hand, his rifle in the other, resting on his lap as he stared silently into the distance. The shirt he once wore was now gone, replaced by a Seminole straight shirt, colorful beads around his neck. Ghost Bear was there next to Topher holding a rifle of his own, his face painted for battle, black handprints stamped on his horse's chest. And surrounding Topher and Ghost Bear was an army of Seminole warriors, many on horseback, some on foot, all ready for war.

Topher continued his silent vigil, remembering his loved ones, reflecting on life's journey that had brought him to this moment. He took a deep, thoughtful breath, then exhaled slowly as he looked around admiringly at the Seminoles. He knew none of them, yet in some way he knew them all.

On the opposite side of the battlefield stood the U.S. Army's Fourth Infantry Division, Major John Thomason in command. Major Thomason and his mounted officers watched transfixed, a grim admiration on their faces.

As conflict loomed, adversaries watched and waited from opposite sides, finding comfort in the pre-war tranquility—calmness before the storm. After several minutes of quiet stillness, Ghost Bear raised his rifle slowly and held it aloft, a sense of duty and purpose born of the many injustices his people and those like his had suffered at the hands of the yellow hair. With each breath filling him further with pride, Ghost Bear let out a chilling war cry that echoed across the battlefield like a spirit possessed … and the Seminoles charged. They hurled themselves across the clearing into battle, in honor of Crow Dog and Joseph Tree, in tribute to Great Elk, and Mercy and Mamé, and so many others … and for Black Fox. As the Seminoles charged into battle, the owl fixed its gaze on the warriors for a moment, then spread its wings and took flight, soaring over the battlefield before disappearing over the lush forest canopy.

And so it was in the fall of 1857 that

Christopher Narcisse joined the fight against slavery, tyranny and oppression—in the fight for freedom. Amidst a sea of charging warriors, he stormed with Ghost Bear across the battlefield, racing headlong toward his destiny …

Acknowledgements

Thank you to all my family and friends over the past several years for believing in my original screenplay idea and giving me the encouragement and support to see this book project through.

An extra special thanks to my incredible partner and best friend Abby Bordner.

Special thanks to my Launch Team! You all know who you are.

Thank you to Maxann Dobson at Polished Pen for her stellar, insightful editing.

Thank you to Emily Tippetts for her advice and book formatting services.

Made in the USA
San Bernardino, CA
14 October 2018